DRAGON WARS

◆ DEATH IN THE DESERT ◆

— BOOK 11 —

CRAIG HALLORAN

Dragon Wars: Death in the Desert - Book 11

By Craig Halloran

★★★★★

Copyright © 2019 by Craig Halloran

Dragon Wars is a registered trademark

Amazon Edition

TWO-TEN BOOK PRESS

PO Box 4215, Charleston, WV 25364

ISBN eBook: 978-1-946218-86-5

ISBN Paperback: 979-8-696165-19-6

ISBN Hardback: 978-1-946218-87-2

WWW.DRAGONWARSBOOKS.COM

Publisher's Note

This book is a work of fiction. Names, characters, places, and incidents either are the product of the author's imagination or are used fictitiously, and any resemblance to actual persons, living or dead, events, or locales is entirely coincidental.

❀ Created with Vellum

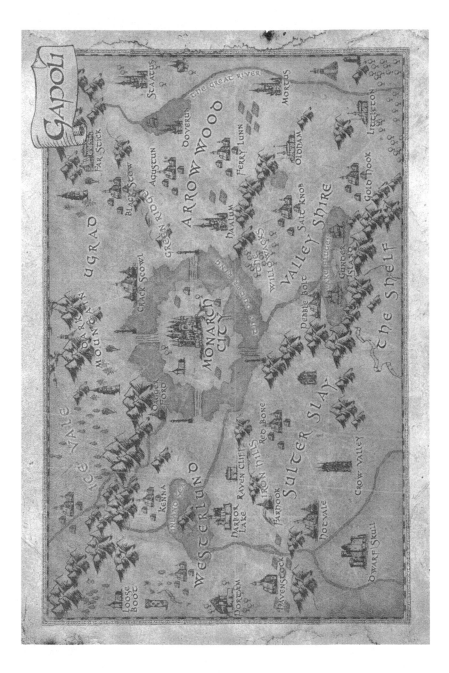

THE FALLS AT THE OUTER RING

IN THE SHADOWS cast by the Iron Hills and the drizzling rain, Dyphestive sat on his backside along with the other members of his group, his hands on top of his head. His jaw clenched as he ground his teeth. His eyes were on the leader of the Doom Riders, Drysis. He'd killed the woman with his own hands, and yet she lived again.

"This isn't possible," he mumbled to Grey Cloak.

Grey Cloak, sitting beside him with his fingers locked on top of his head, quietly replied, "You should know by now, anything is possible. Don't worry. I'll think of something."

As soon as the blood brothers had crested the climb from the depths of Thannis, they'd found themselves face-to-face with Drysis, Scar, Shamrok, and Ghost. The four Doom Riders were in full control. Zora, Jakoby,

Leena, and Gorva were on their knees, disarmed, with their hands tied behind their backs. Razor lay on the ground near the base of the Iron Hills, taking short breaths and wheezing. He was as pale as a ghost. A crossbow bolt protruded from his shoulder and belly, and he bled.

"Heh-heh-heh," Scar laughed in his rugged voice as he approached Dyphestive and squatted in front of him. He took off his dyed-red leather skull mask, revealing his broad face littered with ugly scars. "My brother Iron Bones has returned. Drysis, please allow me to kill him."

Dyphestive sneered at Scar. "In a fair fight, you don't stand a chance."

"We'll see about that." Scar punched Dyphestive in the jaw. His brows knitted together as he stood up and walked away, rubbing his fist.

"We won't be killing anyone yet," Drysis said. Her head was shaved, and her skin was as white as a sheet. Blue spidery veins showed all over her face. She wore the same armor as always, black leather fashioned like dragon scales, the same as the other Doom Riders. Her left arm was covered in chain mail. Her right eye was as black as a pearl, and she wore an eye patch over her left. She carried her pump-action crossbow loaded with four bolts on her shoulder. She glanced at Razor. "But one of them will die soon enough."

Razor lifted his head and spat. "You shot me like a

coward. All because I took your man apart." He looked at Ghost.

The Doom Rider in a dyed-blue skull mask was being tended to by Shamrok. Shamrok was attaching Ghost's right leg with a heavy needle and thread. Ghost held his lower left arm, which had been cut off at the elbow.

"Or whatever that thing is." Razor chuckled. "I took his arm and his leg off. You should have seen me, Jakoby. I was brilliant." His head collapsed onto the dirt.

"Razor!" Jakoby moved toward his fallen friend.

Scar kicked Jakoby to the ground. "Stay put, or I'll split your skull open!"

"He needs attention!" Dyphestive shouted. He started to rise.

Drysis pointed her crossbow at him. "Iron Bones, you shouldn't worry. Soon you will be in worse shape than he is."

Grey Cloak pulled his brother down. "Let me do the talking."

Dyphestive shrugged away his brother's hand and rose to his feet. "It's me you want, Drysis. Leave them out of it. Let them go."

The corner of her mouth turned up. "Do you think this is about revenge? The mere thought is beneath me. Look at me, Iron Bones. My body is everlasting now. How can you kill someone who has already died?"

"You'd be surprised," Grey Cloak muttered.

Dyphestive started toward Razor. "I'm going to help him."

Drysis put the tip of her crossbow against Zora's head. "Take one more step, and I'll turn her into food for the gourn." She pushed Zora's head back. "Don't trifle with me. Sit down," she commanded.

He stopped, moved back, and took his seat by Grey Cloak. His blood simmered inside his veins. He looked Drysis in the eye. "You are vile."

"Thank you." Drysis lifted her crossbow from Zora's forehead. "If you don't want your companions to be fed to the gourn"—she glanced back at the horselike beasts with scales like dragons and smoke for breath—"you will turn the Figurine of Heroes over to me. That is mercy. I suggest you take it."

"We didn't recover the figurine," Grey Cloak said. "We barely made it out with our lives."

"Interesting," Drysis said. She pointed the crossbow at Zora again. "Are you sure that is your final answer?"

"You've searched us. I don't have it. We don't have it. Check everything," Grey Cloak said. "I swear it."

"You're a fast-talker, elf. Scar, search him head to toe... thoroughly," Drysis added.

"As you wish." Scar strolled over to Grey Cloak and gave him a swift kick to the gut.

Grey Cloak groaned as he doubled over.

Scar yanked him up by the hair and ripped his cloak

off. He ran his large callused hands through the cloak and flapped it in the wind. He tossed it aside. From there, he proceeded to firmly pat Grey Cloak down all over. He emptied coins from his trouser pockets, tore off his shirt, and stomped on it. "Drysis, he doesn't have anything on him."

"Search them all, their horses and gear as well." She pushed Zora away with the tip of her crossbow. "Start with this one."

Scar offered Zora a crooked smile. "I'd be glad to." He started toward Zora, tripped on Grey Cloak's foot, and stumbled down on one knee. He jumped up with sword in hand and came at Grey Cloak, his sword raised. "I'll kill you!"

"No! We need him alive," Drysis said. "Do as I asked!"

Scar sheathed his sword and spit. "I'll get you." He shifted his glance to Dyphestive. "I'll get you both."

Dyphestive and Grey Cloak watched Scar search the others and their horses. They spoke to one another in whispers.

Dyphestive said, "They are going to take us back to Black Frost, aren't they?"

"Let them," Grey Cloak said. "We only need to get them away from our friends."

"Agreed. We'll find another way out," Dyphestive replied as he stared at Drysis's back, "even if I have to kill her again."

Scar emptied the last saddlebag and kicked his boots through the contents. "Nothing, Drysis. Now what?"

Drysis set her intense gaze on the blood brothers. "I'm not a fool. I know when I'm being lied to." She lifted her black eye patch, revealing a blazing-blue gemstone. "Bring me the elf."

2

SCAR LOCKED both of Grey Cloak's arms behind his back in a chicken wing. Drysis reached out, grabbed his chin, and held him fast.

"You have a very strong grip for a lady," Grey Cloak said. "Your fingers are as strong as iron. Have you ever considered being a masseuse?"

"Be silent, and look into my eye," Drysis commanded.

"It's a better option than smelling your breath." He glanced into her eye and melted. "Oh, that's pretty."

"Don't look in her devil eye! Don't look," Razor sputtered.

The blade master's voice sounded like it was leagues away. Grey Cloak felt his entire inner being sucked into the warmth offered by Drysis's gemstone eye. His limbs loosened, and he felt as light as a feather.

"Tell me, where is the Figurine of Heroes?" she asked.

He stared back with a languid look. "Oh that." He wanted to tell her everything. His thoughts, his fears, his love for Zora. He smacked his lips. "Well, it's somewhere in the world, now isn't it?" He giggled.

Drysis's voice became a seductive purr. "But you do know where it is, don't you, dear Grey Cloak?"

His head swayed side to side. "Oh, I know everything. Did you know that?"

Her fingers tightened on his chin. "Grey Cloak, you are resisting. The more you resist, the harder it will become. Now tell me about the figurine. Where did you put it?"

"In my pocket."

"It's the devil's eye! Don't look at it!" Razor shouted from what sounded far away.

"Tell the truth," she said.

"I am. It's in my pocket."

"I searched all of his pockets," Scar said. "You saw it."

"Which pocket, Grey Cloak?" she asked.

He felt her thoughts drilling into his. The gemstone and she were one, prying open his mind. He clenched his jaw and shook his head. Tiny needles pierced his mind. He flung his head back and bopped Scar in the chin. "Guh!"

Drysis's voice became more commanding. "The more you hide, the more you hurt. Tell me where the figure is."

Grey Cloak's eyes rolled up in his head as searing pain

flashed through his skull and down into his extremities. He let out an anguished scream. "Nooooooooooooo!"

"You're killing him! Stop it!" Dyphestive demanded.

Drysis raised her voice. "Where is the Figurine of Heroes, Grey Cloak? Tell me now!"

Grey Cloak's muscles knotted and spasmed. He broke out in sweat all over his body. "Nooooooooooo! Noooooooooo!"

"Tell me or die!" Drysis said.

"Stop it! Please stop it!" Zora pleaded. "It's in his cloak! It's in his cloak!" she said.

Drysis swung her burning gaze toward the half-elf rogue. "It's your life or the truth!"

"I swear it." Tears ran down Zora's cheeks. "It's there."

"Fetch me his cloak," Drysis ordered Scar.

Scar dropped Grey Cloak's trembling form on the ground, where he continued to spasm.

Dyphestive scrambled over to his brother and drew him into his arms. "I have you."

"My everything hurts," Grey Cloak mumbled.

Scar retrieved the cloak and handed it to Drysis.

Her eye glowed as she held it up and inspected it. "I see this is no ordinary cloak. It contains many secrets."

Grey Cloak turned his head toward her with his teeth clattering together. He watched as she drew the Figurine of Heroes from one of the secret pockets. His heart sank, but he wasn't finished yet. He summoned the figurine's words of power to mind and quietly uttered them. *Osid-ayan-umra-shokrah-ha!* Nothing happened. He tried again. *Osid-ayan-umra-shokrah-ha!*

Drysis gingerly palmed the figurine and flipped her eye patch down. "Now we have everything we came for." She tossed the cloak to the ground. "Mission accomplished."

"Well done, oh mighty Drysis," Scar said. "What are your orders?"

"Firmly bind Grey Cloak and Iron Bones. We'll take all of their gear and horses with us."

Scar put on his mask. "As you command."

Grey Cloak's tremors began to subside. He looked at Zora. Tears streaked her face.

"It's all right," he said.

Zora swallowed the lump in her throat. "I'm so sorry."

"You aren't to blame. You did your best. We all did."

Scar and Shamrok used chains to bind Grey Cloak and Dyphestive. They shackled them by the wrists and ankles.

Scar put a heavy hand on Iron Bones's shoulder. "Remember these? It's going to be a joy draggin' you back to Dark Mountain."

"Impossible! Impossible!" Razor said when Ghost limped by. His arm and leg were reattached. "Impossible. Let me finish him." Razor's head dropped to the ground again, and his eyelids fluttered and closed.

Scar and Shamrok tethered Grey Cloak and Dyphestive to the horses.

"What about them?" Scar asked about the remaining members of Talon.

Drysis climbed onto her gourn. "We don't have time to waste if they decide to mount a rescue mission. Even if they did, it would be their deaths. Hence, we might as well kill them now."

Scar drew his sword. "As you wish."

"What?" Dyphestive shouted. "You're going to kill them in cold blood? You cowards!"

"Let us die with steel in our palms!" Gorva demanded. "Fight us warrior to warrior!"

"For the Monarchy! I won't die on my knees!" Jakoby started to rise. Leena joined him.

Drysis pointed her crossbow at Jakoby. "Save your bravado for the other side of the Flaming Fence." She squeezed the trigger and fired.

Grey Cloak screamed, "Noooooooooooo!"

3

LEENA SNATCHED the crossbow bolt out of the air. Somehow, she'd slipped her bonds and caught the projectile inches from Jakoby's heart.

"Impressive." Drysis pumped the handle on her crossbow, rotating another bolt in place, ready to fire. She aimed at Zora, who was farthest from Leena. "You might catch one, but no one is quick enough to catch the others."

Dyphestive lowered his shoulder and rammed into the back flank of Drysis's gourn. The beast reared halfway and swung around. Drysis leaned back and pulled on the reins, keeping herself from being slung from the saddle.

The gourn lowered its head and rammed Dyphestive to the ground. It pinned the young man down with one of its lionlike paws. It sank its claws into his chest and breathed hot smoky breath in his face.

Drysis shot Dyphestive in the thigh. The bolt went clean through. "You can limp all the way back to Dark Mountain."

Dyphestive looked at her with clenched jaws. "Fine with me. Just leave my friends alone."

"You aren't in any position to give orders."

"No, but they'll do as I ask." He stretched his neck out. "Jakoby, I need all of you to swear on your lives that you won't pursue us. Promise me, for all of your sakes!"

Sweat ran down the side of Jakoby's face, and with a defeated look, he said, "I swear it." He looked at the others. "We all do. Agreed?"

Zora, Leena, and Gorva nodded.

"You will have no interference from us on your journey back to Dark Mountain," Jakoby added.

"His words mean nothing," Scar said. "Let's kill them."

Grey Cloak spoke up. "He is a Monarch Knight. He will not break his vow." He stared down Scar. "Unlike you, our friends have honor. They will keep their promise to us and let us be. We only ask that you let them live. Look at them. They have no weapons. You're leaving them destitute. They are harmless."

Drysis reached into her quiver and reloaded the empty slots of her crossbow. She slung the crossbow over her shoulder. "Bind the quick one up again," she said, looking at Leena. "Use the chains on all of them."

Scar and Shamrok did as she commanded.

Meanwhile, Dyphestive climbed back to his feet.

Grey Cloak eyed the bolt sticking out of his leg. "You aren't going to be able to walk with that."

"Yes, I will," Dyphestive said. With gritted teeth, he slowly pulled the bolt free from his thigh.

"Drysis, at least let us bandage it," Grey Cloak pleaded, "or he'll bleed to death."

"Do what you will, but you won't receive any help from me."

Grey Cloak spied his drab-looking gray cloak and his shirt on the muddy ground. He stretched as far as he could while tethered to the dragon horse. He leaned over, and his fingertips were just long enough to snag the cloak and his shirt. He winked at Dyphestive and bandaged the leg wound with his shirt. He slung the cloak over his brother's shoulders. "For the fever that is sure to come."

Dyphestive huddled under the cloak and stooped over. He nodded. "Thank you, brother."

Once finished, all of the Doom Riders mounted up. Ghost towed Talon's horses and gear with him. He sat at an angle in his saddle and fought to get his once-severed leg in the stirrup.

Grey Cloak cast a look at Zora and the others. Scar and Shamrok chained them together so that one couldn't walk without falling over the other. They weren't going anywhere, not without help.

I don't even think I could get out of that.

Zora's shoulders sagged, and her chin dipped to her chest. She managed to lift her eyes and mouth the words to Grey Cloak. "I'm sorry."

Leading from the front, Drysis said, "Onward."

The gourn moved forward. The tether that tied the blood brothers by the waist to the beasts' saddles drew tight and jerked them forward. They both took one last look at their friends, nodded, and shuffled down the muddy road.

The march moved at a brutal pace with Dyphestive limping the entire way. Even with the brothers' long strides, they struggled to keep up.

Grey Cloak could have jogged, as it wouldn't have been a problem for him, but he opted to mimic the troubled efforts of his brother.

The weaker they think we are, the better.

Hence, the bare-chested elf stumbled along, keeping his lips sealed for a change, exchanging hopeful glances with his brother from time to time while trying to figure out the best way to escape. They had to take into consideration four Doom Riders, not to mention their fire-breathing beasts, which were every bit as dangerous, if not more so.

It didn't take him long to get a feel for the Doom Riders either. The rugged band of warriors were tireless. They didn't slouch in their saddles, and they gave no regard to the damp and miserable weather. They used coarse language and mocked Dyphestive at every turn, especially Scar. The red-masked Doom Rider towed Dyphestive and pulled him to the ground and dragged him several times throughout the day.

Dyphestive never spoke a word, but his eyes burned with hatred. Scar's burned right back.

"Drysis, this pace is too slow," Scar said as he shifted in his saddle. "It will take weeks to ride to Dark Mountain. It would be faster if we trotted. They can keep up or be dragged."

"Your complaints tire me," Drysis said without so much as a backward glance. "If you wish to arrive at Dark Mountain without us, I suggest you go ahead."

Scar grumbled behind his mask.

"What's that?" she asked.

"Nothing." Scar dug his boot heels into the ribs of his gourn.

The beast lunged forward and jerked Dyphestive by the rope around his waist and off his feet. He face-planted.

Scar dragged him too fast for him to regain his feet. "Hah, Iron Bones, remember this? Good times!"

It went like that off and on all day, and even when night came, they didn't stop to rest.

4

IT WAS a breezy afternoon as they headed north through Westerlund, making a straight line for the Ugrad territory. The Outer Ring winds came from the east, bending the tall grass in the plains downward. They stayed on a rocky stretch of road with ankle-deep wagon ruts crisscrossing through it.

Grey Cloak licked his dried lips. He hadn't had a drop of water, and he didn't ask for any either. His belly rumbled but not nearly as loudly as Dyphestive's, which caused Shamrok to turn and chuckle. It didn't help that he had gained a greater appreciation for food since he'd woken from his coma, which had subdued him in Sulter Slay.

I could eat an entire pig now.

But that wasn't the worst of it. His feet burned like fire. He'd lost his boots in the Ruins of Thannis and had been barefoot ever since. Needless to say, his elven feet weren't accustomed to the hard travel, and as much as he tried to avoid jagged sandrocks, he still hit them all of the time. His feet bled.

Dyphestive came closer, keeping his head down. "How are you holding up?"

"I'll make it."

"It's still far off, and I don't think we'll stop," Dyphestive added.

Grey Cloak nodded. "I know. They aren't fools. If they keep up this endless march, they know we won't have time to plan an escape. As if these shackles digging into our ankles weren't bad enough."

His brother nodded. "They aren't taking any chances. Grey, I don't want to go back. I'd rather die."

"What do you suggest we do?"

Dyphestive looked at the horses with all of their gear. The Iron Sword and the Rod of Weapons were clearly visible. "If we can get our weapons, we can fight."

"Or die," Grey Cloak added. His gaze slid over his cloak.

There was something that he didn't quite understand. When Drysis had retrieved the figurine, she'd overlooked all of the other items that he'd stuffed in his pockets. They held treasure from Thannis, but even with the eye, she'd somehow missed it.

"So, how does my cloak feel?"

"I feel better with it than without it."

Scar turned in his saddle. "Gum up, you two!" He towed Dyphestive farther away from his brother. "Not another word, or I'll drag you again."

Grey Cloak met the man's intense gaze and turned away.

His thoughts wandered back to Zora and the other members of Talon. He had a sinking feeling that if he and Dyphestive were taken back to Dark Mountain, he would never see any of them again. He pictured all of them bound in chains. They had a defeated look in their eyes.

Certainly, they can slip those chains. I only hope they slip them before someone else finds them first. If they die, it will be my fault. He stared at the backs of the Doom Riders in front of him. *No, Grey Cloak, it will be theirs. Remember that.*

With dusk on the horizon and storm clouds rolling overhead, the skies filled with thunder and started to blacken and purple. The road took a downward slope into a rocky hill valley. In the distance were fields, farmland, and villages, but not a single traveler crossed their path. Grey Cloak was certain that various people of Westerlund saw them coming and quickly veered off the road.

He saw no help in sight, and then the rain came. It started with heavy raindrops that were broadly scattered and splashed down inches apart, but ahead, he could see heavier streaks of rain pouring down from the clouds. Lightning flashed, and thunder popped in loud booms, and the hard rain came down.

The Doom Riders continued the slow trek down the sloppy road as if the coming storm was nothing more than a gentle breeze on a sunny day. They plodded along unfettered by the harsh elements.

Scanning the new, rugged terrain, Grey Cloak realized it would be the best opportunity to escape. They could hide in the rocks, separate the Doom Riders, and try to take them down individually.

Anything is possible.

He considered his options. *Distract the Doom Riders. Cut the tethers. Steal a horse and ride. Of course, the gourn are much faster than normal horses. Hmmm... what can I use for a distraction? Perhaps I can have Dyphestive stir things up. I can use my wizardry as well. It should be enough to claim our weapons.*

He wiped rain from his chin.

When it's darkest and the rain's the heaviest, that will be the perfect time to strike. All I need to do now is communicate the plan to Dyphestive.

The large raindrops picked up in volume, soaking everyone from head to toe in seconds. The wagon wheel ruts filled with water, and the gourn sank ankle-deep in the mud, their feet making a sucking sound as they came out.

The cool mud seeped between Grey Cloak's toes, relieving the burning sensation in his feet. He trudged along, angling closer to Dyphestive, and nodded, trying to grab his brother's attention.

Drysis came to a stop, forcing the other Doom Riders to

stop abruptly. She sat tall in the saddle, peering at the bend in the rocks that loomed above them.

"Did you see something?" Scar asked as his hand fell to his sword. "I can scout ahead."

Grey Cloak and Dyphestive crept behind the gourn and craned their necks.

The roadway was clear as far as Grey Cloak could see, and the passage wasn't anything more extraordinary than what they'd already been through.

What is going on?

A booming thunderclap was followed by a bright lightning bolt that pierced the ground on the road ahead. Grey Cloak's jaw dropped at the sight of a warrior standing at the top of the hill with a sword drawn and held to the sky. The image only lasted a moment. Lightning flashed again, and the warrior was gone, vanished with the light that was swallowed up by the darkness.

"I saw it!" Scar said.

"I saw it too," Shamrok added as he pulled his sword. "We should scout it out, Drysis."

"No, we don't know what lies behind those rocks. If they want us, they will have to come to us."

Lightning flashed, and thunder boomed. The warrior in full-metal armor appeared on the road, as bright and striking as the sun. Grey Cloak's heart leaped in his chest. There was no mistaking the long, wet tangles of red hair. It was Anya.

5

GREY CLOAK WIPED the water from his eyes and caught Dyphestive looking at him with his jaw hanging. They'd been told that Anya—the last of the Sky Riders—had been killed over a decade ago. The last time he'd seen her was outside the Wizard Watch in the elven lands of Arrowwood, and no one had seen her since. Yet there she was, marching down the sloppy road straight toward them with Storm in hand.

Scar spoke loudly, "Who is that?"

"I don't know, but I like that red hair," Shamrok said. "I bet she came to give me a kiss."

Anya stopped thirty paces away. She stared the Doom Riders down.

"She wears the armor of a Sky Rider," Shamrok

commented, "but all of the Sky Riders are dead. Who are you, woman?"

Anya didn't bat an eye. Thunder boomed. Lightning streaked behind her.

The sight of Anya charged Grey Cloak's blood. He started to draw forth the wizard fire. He caught Dyphestive's attention and said, "This is it."

"Move, woman, or we will run you over," Scar said.

Anya held her sword in front of her. It was a Sky Rider's blade with a cross guard shaped like wings. "This is the end of the road, Doom Riders," she said.

"She talks!" Scar said.

"And boldly. I like it," Shamrok added. "Why don't you put away that length of steel and join me in the saddle, pretty thing?"

Anya looked him in the eye. "I don't ride with dead men."

Scar and Shamrok erupted in hearty chuckles.

"I think you've found your bride-to-be, Shamrok. She's perfect for you," Scar said.

Shamrok nodded. "Once I break her, she'll be perfect."

Drysis's voice cut like a knife. "Bridle your tongues. What do you want?"

"I came for Grey Cloak and Dyphestive and to put an end to you," Anya replied.

"A bold statement for a warrior who walks alone, but you aren't alone, are you?" Drysis said. She flipped up her eye patch and scanned the hillsides. "Interesting. I don't see any allies. Perhaps they are on the other side of the rocks."

"I swear by my sword, I'm the only person here." Anya lifted her blade skyward. A bolt of lightning streaked down and struck the metal. Her green eyes burned like torches. "Prepare to die!"

"I'll handle this witch!" Shamrok said. He spurred his gourn forward into a charge. The sudden move jerked Grey Cloak's waist forward, but he fought and kept on his feet.

The Doom Rider and gourn bore down on the woman standing in their path.

Grey Cloak shouted ahead, "Anya, move!"

Anya stood her ground. Her glimmering Sky Blade flashed. She decapitated the gourn. The beast plowed over her, tossing Shamrok from the saddle.

He rolled back to his feet. Shamrok stared down at his dead beast and dropped to his knees. "You chopped my gourn's head off. You'll pay for that!"

Grey Cloak jumped toward Anya and shielded her with his body. She was pinned underneath the fallen beast, which had smoke streaming out of its neck. "Anya, it's good to see you! That was incredible!"

She wormed her way out from underneath the beast. "Can't you find a better time to chat?" She pulled a dagger and severed his tether. "Duck!"

Grey Cloak dropped flat on the ground. Ghost's sword sliced over his head. He followed up with a deadly downward chop. Grey Cloak spread his legs, exposing the chains shackling his feet. Ghost's blade cut clean through them.

"Thank you!" he said.

Ghost sliced his other sword at Grey Cloak's head. Steel rang against steel.

Anya blocked it. "Try me, Doom Rider!"

Shamrok flanked her, both hands filled with steel. "He doesn't talk, but I do!"

Anya pushed Ghost backward.

"Kill the woman, but we must keep Grey Cloak alive!" Drysis said as she unslung her crossbow from her shoulder.

Grey Cloak and Anya stood back-to-back with Ghost and Shamrok circling them.

"Four blades to your one. Perhaps you should bring more the next time you mount a rescue," Grey Cloak said.

"Why would I do that when your tongue is as sharp as any blade I've ever carried?" she replied.

"It sounds like you missed me, Anya."

"I didn't even know you were gone."

Shamrok chuckled. "So, you are Anya, the last of the Sky Riders. And all these years, we thought you were dead. Well, I'll be sure to keep the rumors of your death intact, Red."

"I don't think so." Anya sprang away from Grey Cloak, separating herself from the circle, and unleashed a strike at

Shamrok. Steel flashed against steel, and sparks flew in the rain as he blocked her with both of his swords.

Ghost moved toward Anya.

Grey Cloak blocked his path. "That's between them. This is between us."

The rangy Doom Rider tilted his head to one side.

"That's right. You can't kill me, so what are you going to do?" Grey Cloak asked with a grin.

Ghost stuck his swords in the mud, sprang like a cat, and tackled Grey Cloak.

"Zooks, I didn't see that coming," Grey Cloak said just before Ghost shoved his face into the messy road.

6

SCAR KEPT his eyes on Dyphestive. "Don't even think about it, Iron Bones." He pulled his sword free from his back scabbard. "Make a move, and I'll run you through."

Dyphestive held the taut rope that tethered him to Scar's gourn. He gave it some slack. "You aren't allowed to hurt me."

"I will if I have to."

The gourn turned its head and spit flames from its mouth.

Dyphestive backed away from the searing heat. He moved to the other side of the gourn and peeked at the battle unfolding between Anya, Grey Cloak, and the Doom Riders.

They need my help!

"Don't get any wise ideas. It will be over for your redheaded friend soon," Scar warned.

"Unlikely. She's a Sky Rider. She draws upon powers that you can't begin to comprehend."

"That was a nice trick with the lightning, but we've killed our share of Sky Riders over the years and dealt with their methods before," Scar added.

Dyphestive moved forward and stood on the other side of the gourn's head. "It's a shame that's not me and you out there fighting. I'd be stomping you into a mudhole right now."

Scar let out a gravelly chuckle. "You're no match for me, boy."

"I'm younger. I'm stronger." Dyphestive balled up his fists. "And you're scared."

"In your—"

Dyphestive unleashed his hatred and hit the gourn square in the jaw with all of his might. The beast's neck rolled, and its knees gave out beneath it.

Scar rolled backward off the gourn's back and came to his feet, swords drawn, on the other side of the beast. "You're a dead man!"

Dyphestive stretched the chains between his wrist cuffs, growled, and snapped the links apart. "No, you are!" He jumped over the gourn in a single bound and hit Scar like a battering ram.

The two men rolled through the mud like pigs

wallowing in slop. Dyphestive grabbed the man's wrist and twisted the blade out of his hand. Scar chopped down at him with his free sword arm. The pommel of the weapon struck Dyphestive's back. One rolled over the other and back again. Dyphestive shoved his forearm into Scar's neck and pushed him back.

Behind the mask, Scar's eyes were like flames. "I'll kill you! I swear it!" He reversed the grip on his sword and brought it down in a stabbing motion.

Dyphestive twisted away, drew his leg back, and kicked Scar hard in the chest.

"Oof!" Scar went flying backward and lost his sword in the mud. He rolled over and crawled for it.

"No, you don't!" Dyphestive pounced.

He was a foot from landing on Scar's back when the rope around his waist pulled him backward. He rolled onto his backside. The gourn he'd punched towed him away from Scar. He grabbed the rope in both hands, shoved his heels in the mud, and pulled.

"No!"

The gourn stopped in its tracks. It let out a blast of fire, looked back at Dyphestive with eyes like burning flames, and marched on. Dyphestive's heels made new ruts in the road as he was pulled forward. Behind him, Scar gathered his swords from the mud and marched after him.

Scar pointed a sword in Dyphestive's direction. "This is over!"

Unlike his chains, Dyphestive couldn't tear the rope apart. He pulled back with all his might, but the gourn had at least a thousand pounds on him, and there was murder in Scar's eyes. He was going to kill Dyphestive.

Dyphestive searched for a weapon, any kind of weapon. He saw nothing nearby. The train of horses and Talon's gear were far out of reach. The only things he had were mud and rock.

Scar closed in and poised his swords to strike. "I'll see you on the other side of the fence. Maybe we'll be friends then."

Dyphestive snarled, "I don't think so." He flung a handful of mud in Scar's face.

"Gah!" Scar shouted. "Coward!" He stabbed and chopped wildly.

Dyphestive got on his feet and raced toward the unsuspecting gourn. From behind the beast, he vaulted into the saddle and grabbed the reins.

The gourn let out a startled roar. It bucked like a wild mule. Dyphestive tucked his fingers into the saddle and held on for his life. The wild dragon horse jumped five feet off the ground. It danced, galloped, bucked all over the road. Flame and fire blasted out of its mouth and nostrils. It let out high-pitched shrieking whinnies.

He squeezed the beast with his powerful legs and grabbed one side of its horns. It bucked twice more. Dyphestive was launched out of the saddle and landed on the side of the road. He hit hard and rolled up onto one knee. He caught Scar staring him down from a short distance.

The Doom Rider had climbed back into his gourn's saddle. He lifted his sword to the sky. The gourn reared up to a towering height and huffed out a blossom of orange flames. Its front claws came down deep in the mud. It set its eyes on Dyphestive, clawed at the road, snorted out smoke, and charged.

7

GHOST HIT Grey Cloak in the back of the head with a rabbit punch. Grey Cloak stumbled face-first into the mud with spots in his eyes. The Doom Rider dropped both knees into his back, making him sink deeper into the sludge.

Grey Cloak pushed up from his belly. Ghost popped him in the back of the head again.

Whop!

He sagged into the sludge. Ghost's mailed fist might as well have been a hammer. It sent pain streaking down his spine. Ghost pushed off of him and resumed his march toward Anya and Shamrok, who were in the middle of a deadly dance in the rain with their blades.

It was clear that Ghost would move in for the kill. Anya wouldn't stand a chance against the two of them.

"No." Grey Cloak clawed his way out of the mudhole.

His bare feet slipped in the grimy murk. They finally found purchase, and he launched himself into the back of Ghost's legs.

They both went down in a heap of tangled limbs. Ghost cracked his cheek with a hard elbow.

Grey Cloak slipped behind the bigger man and put him in a headlock. "Let's see you get out of this!"

The Doom Rider dropped his hip and tried to fling Grey Cloak off with a hip toss.

Grey Cloak hung on for his life. "You're as strong as a mule, aren't you?" He squeezed harder.

Ghost stood up and stumbled over the road. His limbs were as strong as iron, and the dragon armor he wore made Grey Cloak's fists useless against it. He needed a weapon. Ghost jumped up and flopped onto his back, crushing Grey Cloak beneath him. The soft mud broke Grey Cloak's fall, but he was still being buried beneath the brute.

He held on. *He should be dead. I'm choking him to death. Don't the dead die in this world anymore?* He swallowed a mouthful of mud. "Gack!"

Grey Cloak twisted underneath Ghost and reversed his position so that he was on top of the man's back, crushing his neck with all his might. "Do you even breathe?" he panted.

Ghost lifted his hand and spread out his fingers. Sharp metal fingernails popped out of his gauntlets' fingertips.

"Scary. What are you going to do with those?" Grey Cloak asked.

The Doom Rider slashed Grey Cloak's arms with his metal fingernails.

"Gah!" Grey Cloak released him. "Dirty acorns, you dirty fighter!" He cradled his bleeding limbs. "You're starting to make me mad."

Ghost had every advantage. Armor. Weapons. Grey Cloak didn't have anything to focus his wizard fire through. He needed a weapon of some sort. That was when he noticed Ghost's swords stuck in the ground. He was closer to them than Ghost was.

"Ah-ha!" He dashed for the blades.

Ghost did the same.

Grey Cloak reached the swords a hair quicker, but he only could grab one before Ghost snatched the other. "Blazes, you're fast for a man in full armor," Grey Cloak said with an astonished look. He sliced the sword through the air. "But we are on equal terms now."

The fighters circled.

He beckoned Ghost closer. "Do your worst."

Ghost launched himself at Grey Cloak.

Grey Cloak summoned wizard fire. His blade glowed with bright energy. A bolt of power shot forth and knocked Ghost off his boots.

Anya sidestepped Shamrok's thrust and parried another. She deflected a series of overhand chops and broke away from the melee.

Shamrok let out a gusty laugh in the rain, and a thunderclap followed. "What's the matter, Sky Rider? Are your little arms beginning to tire?"

She filled her lungs with a deep breath and pulled her dagger.

"Your little dagger will be no match for me. I'm bigger. I'm stronger and faster. Surrender, Red, because I'd hate to kill a woman as pretty as you."

"Don't be so sure of yourself. All I've heard from you is talk," she replied as she backed down the road.

Shamrok made a valid point. He was bigger and strong, a fine swordsman too. Her shoulders burned like fire, and her arms had become heavy, but Anya had been in hiding for over ten years, and she was itching for a fight. And in those ten years, she'd practiced her sword craft too.

"Care to try to kill me again?"

"A woman with a death wish. I like it, even though it's a waste of talent." Shamrok charged forward, thrusting his swords at her in an alternating pattern. He chased her up the slope toward the grassy hillside.

Anya spun away from the striking steel, slipped around the pattern of attack, and stuck her dagger in the back of Shamrok's thigh.

He let out a howl and unleashed a decapitating back-swing that she ducked underneath.

Swish!

They exchanged blade blow against blade blow in a storm of steel.

Shamrok's hard, heavy strikes numbed her arms to the shoulders. Anya fought on. In the back of her mind, she wanted to use her wizardry, but she knew the Doom Riders' armor was designed to protect them from it. It wouldn't even leave a mark, but it might hold him back. She would have to beat him on her own.

"You're tired, little woman!" he said, hammering away at her blocking blades with overhanded strikes.

"And you bleed. It will catch up with you."

"Not if I cut you down first," he said.

Anya broke away from the melee and kept her distance. Her shoulders sagged, and she could barely lift her arms. A tingling sensation in her hands throbbed and bit like she could still feel him hitting her.

"Where's your dragon, little girl? Now might be a good time to fly away," Shamrok said.

She wiped her nose across her wrist. "I journey alone."

"A wise move. Any dragon that isn't one of us would be killed in these parts." He shook his head, wicking the rain from his red locks. "Are you certain you want to finish this dance?" He came forward with a limp. "I can show you mercy if you wise up and join us."

She set her eyes on him. "I'd die first."

Shamrok removed his mask. He was a handsome man with a strong jaw and angular features. His piercing eyes met hers. "So be it, then."

8

DYPHESTIVE LOWERED HIS SHOULDER. The gourn ran right over him. Its back hooves stomped his chest and crushed his back into the ground. The beast charged on, turned, and prepared for another pass.

"How'd that feel, Iron Bones?" Scar shouted.

He stood in the ankle-deep sludge and faced his attacker. The gourn huffed out a mushroom of flame, sizzling the rain and creating a cloud of rising steam. Dyphestive cracked his neck from side to side as the mud slid away from the cloak. He removed it and held it out with two hands and flapped it in the wind. "Let's try that again!"

The gourn clawed at the mud, let out a roar, and charged.

At the last moment, Dyphestive tossed the cloak in the gourn's face and dove to the side.

The cloak covered the gourn's head like a sack. The gourn shook its head, but the cloak didn't come free.

Scar freed his feet from the stirrups and leapt from the saddle on top of Dyphestive. Their tremendous bodies crashed together, and down they went. They locked up like lizards and tried to kill each other.

"I'm going to kill you!" Scar headbutted Dyphestive in the nose and punched his ribs. "Tonight, you die!"

Dyphestive threw an elbow and busted Scar's ribs.

"Hah! My armor protects me." Scar grabbed a handful of Dyphestive's hair and pulled his face down into a knee. Scar busted him in the face three times. He hit him hard, high and low. His fists smote him like blacksmith hammers.

Dyphestive fought his way to his knees and covered himself with his meaty arms like a crab. He started blocking Scar's heavy blows. "You can't hurt me!" He stuck his chin out. "Try if you can!"

Scar hauled back and hit him in the jaw with everything he had.

Dyphestive's head rocked backward. He rolled it back forward, spit out a tooth, and grinned. "You'll have to do better than that, little man."

"I will!" Scar started punching him in the face as hard as he could. "I will! Curse you! Your head is as hard as an anvil!"

Dyphestive let him punch away. Every blow stung, but that was about it.

Scar sucked in a breath and lifted his hands before his face. He tried to bend his fingers and gaped. "They're broken."

"What a shame." Dyphestive's own hand swallowed one of Scar's fists and started to crush it.

"Guh!" Scar cried out. The metal finger guards bent. Bones broke. "Stop that!"

Dyphestive balled up his other fist and slugged Scar in the jaw so hard his mask came off. The Doom Rider crawled through the mud on his belly away from Dyphestive. Dyphestive grabbed his leg and towed him back.

Scar snaked a dagger out of his scabbard and lunged at Dyphestive. Dyphestive caught Scar by the wrist. The towering men pushed back and forth, trying to gore one another. Dyphestive's great strength prevailed. He turned the dagger toward Scar's abdomen and started to press it forward.

Scar locked eyes with him and said with defiance, "I hate you!"

"I hate you more." Dyphestive plunged the dagger deep and watched the hatred in Scar's burning eyes diminish.

Dagger in hand, he turned on his knees and found himself looking up into the face of Drysis. "I hope you're ready to die again."

She pulled the trigger on her crossbow and shot him in the chest. "I don't think so."

Grey Cloak watched Ghost rise from the ground with a stupefied look on his face. The Doom Rider's chest plate was smoking, but he didn't slow a bit. His long, slender limbs carried him with fluid ease across the sloppy road. "You aren't flesh and blood. Great. Is anyone flesh and blood these days but us?" He shrugged. "Oh well, I guess I'll have to do this the hard way."

The warriors collided. Grey Cloak matched Ghost stroke for stroke. Sparks jumped off their steel.

His mind raced in the course of battle. *How do you kill the dead?*

Razor had taken the Doom Rider down only to see him be put back together again. And clearly Razor was better with a length of sharp steel. Hence, Grey Cloak parried, searching for a weakness. Ghost had a hitch in his foot-work, and he used his sword arm that hadn't been severed.

Attack the leg.

Grey Cloak wrapped both hands on his sword handle and pressed the attack. He thrust, chopped, parried, and countered.

Ghost matched every move he made with a tireless sword arm and effortless ease.

With his lungs starting to burn and his sword arm tiring, Grey Cloak faked a jab to the shoulder and lunged for the bad knee.

Ghost sidestepped the move and slashed at Grey Cloak's neck.

He jerked away and felt the tip of his ear come off. "Bloody biscuits, you won't make this easy, will you?" He backpedaled.

Ghost kept coming.

"Say something, you silent devil!" He renewed a charge of power and sent a blast from the sword into the Doom Rider's chest.

Ghost sprang over the energy bolt and tackled Grey Cloak.

Not this again.

Winded and tired, he wrestled for his life only to find himself pinned down by his shoulders again. This time, Ghost's armored fingers locked around his throat and squeezed.

Grey Cloak reached up and pushed the man's chin back. He felt himself sinking into the mud and losing his breath. His fingers caught Ghost's mask, and he tore it off. *Gads!*

Ghost wasn't a man but a woman, an elven woman with striking features and jet-black hair. Her sorcerous eyes were black, her skin pasty and pale, and she had a star-shaped birthmark on her cheek. She was an unnatural beauty, her skin cracked by time and filled with blue veins like Drysis's.

"What are you anyway?" Grey Cloak uttered as he sank deeper into the slop.

Ghost didn't answer. Her powerful grip choked off his air.

His vision began to fade into darkness. He let out a garbled, "Nooo."

9

ANYA'S STRENGTH and sword skill kept her intact, but she wasn't a match for the bigger and stronger Shamrok. The Doom Riders were renowned warriors, every bit as gifted as Riskers and Sky Riders without the power of wizardry from bonding with dragons. They were natural-born killers and tireless hunters, fearless and menacing. She'd never faced any man like them.

"Getting tired, pretty thing?" Shamrok gloated as he poked his swords at her belly.

As agile as a cat, she skipped away from what could have been lethal blows. She parried with two arms, barely knocking his swords aside. He was wearing her down.

"Stop!" she said.

Shamrok stopped his advance and tilted his head. He

lowered his swords by his sides. "Go ahead. Catch your breath. I'm enjoying this."

"I can see that." She brushed her rain-soaked locks from her eyes and rolled her shoulders. Her dragon armor, normally light, felt heavy. Everything was. Her shoulders were tight knots, and the muscles between her shoulder blades burned. "I'll admit, you are a very impressive fighter, but you have two swords, and I only have one. Do you care to even the odds?"

"Is that your dying request?"

She nodded and caught her breath.

"So be it." Shamrok tossed his sword aside. "Never let it be said that I didn't treat the lady fairly. I'm a gentleman after all."

"I doubt that."

He shrugged. "You're right. Shall we resume our final dance?"

She lifted a finger, dropped to a knee, and puked to her side. She wiped her mouth and stood back up. "I'm ready now."

"Whoa, you really are fighting your guts out. Respect. On with it, then." He advanced.

Anya turned on the offense. Now that he didn't have a second sword, she could cut through his defenses. She poked at his shoulders and his knees, sending him backpedaling for his life. Shamrok stumbled in the mud and fell to one knee.

She went in for the killing stroke, but Shamrok recovered with a backswing that would have cut through both of her knees. She hopped high and flipped over him. His gaze caught hers as she looked down at him. She landed before he could turn. With her back to his, she delivered the killing stroke, jamming her Sky Blade with a backward thrust through his back and into his heart.

Shamrok died in an instant. Anya plopped down on both knees, gasping for breath. Her body trembled. She'd won. It was over.

Ghost's strong fingers did the job, cutting off Grey Cloak's air supply. He drifted into a state of darkness.

She might not be trying to kill me, but it sure feels like it. Zooks, I'd hate to go like...

Suddenly, her grip slackened. Grey Cloak opened his heavy eyelids. A black appendage flicked out of nowhere and crashed into Ghost. Her entire body was knocked out of view.

He sucked in a breath and started coughing and hacking. He spit mud out of his mouth and wiped it from his eyes. As his vision cleared, he noticed a familiar face staring down at him.

"How have you been, Grey Cloak?" Streak asked. He stared down at Grey Cloak with bright-yellow eyes, and his pink tongue flicked out of his mouth. "It's been a while, eh?"

Grey Cloak shifted his head in the mud. "Streak? Is that you? Your face is so fat."

"Well, yours is muddy. Here, let me help you up." Streak's tail coiled around Grey Cloak's arm and lifted him out of the pool of mud trying to suck him back in. "You haven't been having a good day, have you?"

"I had her right where I wanted her."

"It didn't look like it to me."

Grey Cloak wiped his eyes. "You try fighting an undead Doom Rider without a weapon and with your arms and your legs shackled. I'd like to see how you do."

"Don't be so sensitive. I'm here to help." Streak swung his head in Ghost's direction.

The Doom Rider had retrieved one of her swords. She faced Streak and Grey Cloak but didn't advance, and with good reason.

Grey Cloak got his first good look at Streak. The runt dragon, who had been little bigger than a bulldog, had blossomed into a middling-sized dragon. His small horns had thickened on the top of his back. His twin black streaks ran down his back and split into two separate tails.

"What have you been eating since you've been gone?"

"Milkshakes."

"What's a milkshake?"

"It's a long story that I'll have to explain later, but it had something to do with that portal thingy. I'll tell you this—milkshakes are delicious, especially served with brownies and soft-serve ice cream. You might want to step back, master. I'm about to torch this lady." The scales around his rib cage expanded.

Ghost drew a razor-sharp dagger in her free hand and charged with a handful of steel.

Streak blasted out a geyser of flame that enveloped Ghost from head to toe. The fiery spray clung to her body, but she still advanced. "What, no screaming? The first time I get to flame someone, and they walk through my fire like they've done it a thousand times before."

"She's dead already." Grey Cloak found Ghost's sword lying in the mud and dug it out. He took a deep breath and launched himself at her.

Ghost turned in time to see him coming, but she wasn't fast enough. Grey Cloak swung.

Slice!

Her flaming head leapt from her shoulders and plopped into the mud. The Doom Rider's body continued its march, made it within five steps of Streak, fell forward, and collapsed.

"Bravo," Streak said. "Bravo."

Anya rushed over to Grey Cloak. "Come on. It's your brother, hurry!"

10

Dyphestive lay on the ground with a crossbow bolt sticking out of his chest. His hand was wrapped around the bolt. He grimaced.

"Don't touch that." Grey Cloak kneeled beside his brother.

"If you say so." Dyphestive sat up. "She shot me point blank, got on her gourn, and rode off."

Grey Cloak glanced at Anya. "Did you see where she went?"

"West," she said.

"We have to catch her. She has the figurine."

"I can help." Dyphestive pushed up to his feet with a grunt. "Let's go get her."

"You need to stay still. You have a bolt in your chest."

Grey Cloak put his arm around Dyphestive's waist. "How are you even standing?"

Dyphestive shrugged. "She aimed for my heart, but I flinched when she shot. It must have missed." He tipped his chin over his shoulder. "See if it's sticking out of my back. It feels like it is. Pull it out."

"What? Are you crazy?" Grey Cloak gave Dyphestive an incredulous look. "That could kill you."

"No, I don't think so."

"I can see the tip of the bolt," Anya said. "I can pull it out."

"Nobody is pulling anything out!" Grey Cloak said.

Streak wandered through the rain and joined the group. "How's it going, Dyphestive?"

Dyphestive's pale face lit up. "Streak? Is that you?"

"I know. I've gotten better looking, haven't I?" the dragon said.

"That's not what I was thinking, but yes, there is a slight difference." Dyphestive coughed. His gaze slid over to Grey Cloak. "Brother, we really need to get this thorn out of my chest so I can heal." Dyphestive's eyelids fluttered. His knees buckled, and his full weight came down on Grey Cloak.

"Zooks, you're heavy." He lowered his brother to the ground. "If you weren't such a glutton for punishment, perhaps you wouldn't get shot up so bad." He'd never seen his brother in such bad shape before. The bolt must have done more damage than he'd thought. His mind raced. An idea crossed his mind. "Let me try something."

Grey Cloak fished through the pockets of the Cloak of Legends. In the Ruins of Thannis, he'd packed away many potion vials. He pulled out a clear ancient vial filled with golden liquid. He pulled the cork off with his teeth. "Get ready to pull that bolt out on my signal, Anya."

She nodded. "I'm ready."

Grey Cloak soaked the end of the bolt with a portion of the liquid in the vial. "Drink this," he said to Dyphestive.

"What is it?"

"A vial for healing."

"It sounds good." Dyphestive took the vial from Grey Cloak's hand and drank it down. He looked his brother in the eye. "Do it!"

Grey Cloak nodded at Anya. She ripped the bolt out of his back. Dyphestive stiffened, and Grey Cloak raised his brows.

"Are you well?" Grey Cloak asked.

"It definitely hurts more going out than it does going in." Dyphestive took a breath. "We need to get Drysis."

"I know. She's got a big lead."

Streak flapped his wings. "We can catch her. Get on."

Dyphestive removed the cloak and put it over Grey Cloak's shoulders. "You might need this. Be careful."

"I will." Grey Cloak fetched the Rod of Weapons from their gear on the horses nearby. He mounted Streak. "You know, I'm not the best suited for riding dragons."

"Well, you better get used to it because I love to fly." Streak vaulted into the air. Wings beating in the rain, he jetted through the dark sky.

Grey Cloak held on to the horns on Streak's skull. With his stomach pushed into his back, he fought the urge to hurl. "It's a good thing I haven't eaten lately."

"What?" Streak asked.

"Nothing!" he shouted. "How can you see her in the rain?"

"What I can't see I can smell. Gourns stink. I'm on the trail." The dragon flew low, no more than twenty yards off the ground. They'd only flown a minute when he said, "There she is."

Drysis rode across the grassy plains at a full gallop. Gourn were the fastest four-footed beasts in the world, but they were no match for a flying dragon.

"Cut them off!" Grey Cloak said.

Streak buzzed over Drysis and landed a hundred feet in front of her. Drysis pulled back on the reins and slowed her beast to a walk. The heavy rain died down, but thunder and lightning filled the dark clouds overhead.

Grey Cloak slid off Streak's back. "This is the end of the road for you, Drysis." He charged the Rod of Weapons with wizard fire. The top end blossomed into a glimmering spear point. "I'll make you a deal. Hand over the figurine, and we won't kill you."

"Don't be a fool. Do you really think I fear the likes of you?" She dismounted and brought her crossbow to the front. "All three of my Doom Riders are no match for me."

"Then why did you run?"

"To lure you into my trap by separating you from your pitiful pack." Head high, the undead woman marched forward. "And you walked right into it."

Grey Cloak scanned the plains. He didn't see any help for Drysis, and with the Cloak of Legends on, he felt as confident as ever. "I think it's the other way around."

Drysis stopped twenty feet away. She managed the thinnest of smiles. "Oh, is it?" She flipped up her eye patch, revealing the burning azure gemstone in the socket. "Now you will experience the full power of the Eye of Enthrallment."

"Pretty," Streak said, his tongue hanging out of his mouth. "Sooo pretty."

"Roll over on your back, dragon," she said.

Streak rolled onto his back like a dog, but his eyes never left her eye.

Grey Cloak tried to tear his gaze away. He froze from head to toe. He watched in horror as she raised her crossbow and took aim.

"I've tired of you, Grey Cloak. I can't take any more chances. You leave me no choice but to kill you and your dragon. I'll take all of your heads to Black Frost as proof of your demise."

11

GREY CLOAK TRIED TO SPEAK, but his tongue cleaved to the roof of his mouth.

"What's that, Grey Cloak? You wish to speak? Perhaps you have one last dying request," she said.

His tongue loosened, but the rest of him remained as stiff as a board. "I was going to say that shiny eyeball of yours would make a beautiful engagement ring. Don't you think?"

Her expression filled with disgust. "You jest in your moment of death?"

"No, I'm only delaying the inevitable. Your death."

A grand dragon dropped from the sky and landed behind her.

Drysis turned and found herself facing a chest rich in armored dragon scales. She lifted her gaze and stared right into Cinder's face. She pulled the trigger on her crossbow, firing at the dragon's belly. Cinder covered her in a stream of flame that turned her skin to ash and set her bones on fire while she stood in her suit of armor.

New strength returned to Grey Cloak's limbs. Streak rolled onto all fours. "Cinder! It's about time. What were you doing, waiting for the bus?"

"Anya told me to remain hidden, no matter what," Cinder said politely in his rich voice. He was a magnificent dragon with bright eyes that shined like the sun and golden-flecked scales. "I'm really going to hear about it this time."

"Hah! Cinder, I could hug you!" Grey Cloak rushed the dragon and hugged his massive front paw. "I will hug you!"

"Hey, I didn't get a hug, and I'm your dragon," Streak complained.

Grey Cloak broke away from Cinder and wrapped his arms around Streak's neck. "Sorry, brother."

Streak drummed one of his tails on the grass. "That's better. It looks like dragon power saved the day." He shrugged his wings. "No surprise."

"No complaints," Grey Cloak replied.

Drysis's body burned. Her armor cracked and turned brittle as it burned with wroth heat. Grey Cloak spun his wrist and swung the four-foot-long Rod of Weapons like a club into Drysis's body. Her body collapsed in a heap of flaming bones and ash. The Eye of Enthrallment rolled out of the pile onto the large spot of charred ground.

He picked it up and stared at it. "This beauty might come in handy." His eyes widened. "Oh, the Figurine of Heroes. Where's her gourn?"

Cinder swung his head in the direction of the gourn and gave it a nod. The gourn walked over to Cinder with its head lowered.

"The gourn are misused. They can be as noble as a horse or as vile as their masters," the dragon said.

Grey Cloak searched through the gourn's saddlebags. Elated, he said, "Ah-ha! I have it!" He kissed the Figurine of Heroes and held it up. "Yes! Wait until I show Dyphestive. We can take down the underlings in the Wizard Watch now!"

The two dragons and Grey Cloak headed back to the road. They found Anya sitting on the muddy ground with Dyphestive's head in her lap.

Her face sagged as she petted Dyphestive's cheek. She sobbed when she talked. "He was fine." She gasped. "He gathered those horrid skull masks, gave me a broad smile, turned as white as a sheet, and fell over. He's not breathing. I think Drysis poisoned him."

"No, no, no." Grey Cloak gently slapped Dyphestive's cheek. "You can't be dead, brother. You're a juggernaut. Nothing can stop you." He grabbed Dyphestive by the collar and shook him. "Wake up!"

"Anya," Cinder said gently. "We need to move now, before the storm lifts. Perhaps we can help him at the safe haven. It's the only way."

She sniffed. "Yes, of course. Grey Cloak, help me carry him. I know someone who can possibly help. It's our only choice."

Grey Cloak grabbed Dyphestive under his arms and, with Anya's help, carried him to Cinder, who lowered his huge body to the ground. He was numb inside and out. He couldn't believe it. His friend was dead.

He wrapped Dyphestive up in his cloak and loaded him onto Cinder. "This should keep him warm." He swallowed the lump in his throat. "How far away is this safe haven?"

"Far, but no one can get us there faster than Cinder. You and Streak will have to follow. Gather what you can and catch up." Anya climbed into the grand dragon's saddle. "Hurry!"

"What about my friends? I need to go back for them."

"Your brother needs you now more than ever." She stuck her feet in the stirrups and held onto Dyphestive's body. "Ride the sky, Cinder. Ride the sky!"

"No, wait!"

Grey Cloak fetched the Iron Sword and slid it into a sheath on Cinder's saddle. "Dyphestive would kill me if his sword got lost again."

"I understand." She patted his head. "But that's enough talk. We must move under the cover of the storm. We can't let the Riskers that patrol the skies see us, or this entire rescue mission will be for naught. Fly, Cinder, fly!"

Cinder spread his wings and vaulted into the sky.

"He's fast," Streak said as his gaze followed Cinder. "Not as fast as me, but we better go."

Grey Cloak noticed the Doom Rider masks lying at his feet and picked them up with numb fingers. He wasn't sure exactly why he'd done it, but Dyphestive must have wanted them for some reason. He climbed onto Streak's back and hung on for his life. "Ride the sky."

12

THE IRON HILLS

A DAY EARLIER...

Near the Inland Sea riverbank, Talon was chained and roped together like a ball of twine. All of them wrestled and wriggled in their shackles to no effect.

Jakoby flexed under his chains.

"Ow!" Zora said. "Stop doing that! I told you, when you do that, you pinch me!"

"Sorry, but we need to break these chains." Jakoby twisted his head around to get a look at her. "Aren't you a thief? Can't you squirm out?"

"I'm trying," Zora said in an aggravated tone. "I've never seen chains and ropes like these before. The more we move, the tighter they get." She tried to squeeze her hand out of the cuffs on her wrists. It was a trick she'd performed many times before in the past, but this time she'd met her match. "Leena, how'd you do it before?"

The monk from the Ministry of Hoods remained tight-lipped and carried the same determined look in her intense eyes with her brows knit together.

"We should try to stand and walk," Gorva suggested. The brawny orc woman's muscles knotted in her arms. "We need to move. Possibly shake something loose."

Zora rolled her eyes. "We tried that before, and I ended up on the bottom of the pile. Remember?"

"We'll do it different this time. Everyone, get your backs together," Gorva suggested. "On three. One! Two! Three!"

The four of them rose from their backsides, but Gorva and Jakoby's weight pitched them backward and off balance, and they landed on top of the smaller women.

"Great job, Gorva," Zora said. Her face was smashed into the wet ground with Gorva sitting on top of her. "Will you get off me?"

"I'm trying! No need to yell." Gorva shifted her weight away from Zora, and she ended up smothering Leena beneath her. Leena squirmed away and wound up trapped underneath Jakoby. "This is madness!" Gorva said. "Wherever we move, the chains move with us, like living things."

"We should count our blessings that no goblins have crawled out of the hills to feast on us," Jakoby said. "Now, everyone, calm down."

"Don't tell me to calm down!" Zora said.

"Me either, man!" Gorva agreed.

Leena glared at him.

"Huh-huh-huh," Razor laughed from his spot where he lay on the edge of the hillside. "I might not be able to move, Jakoby, but I'm in better shape than you are. Normally, I'd want to trade places with you, but given the circumstances..." His eyes closed, and his head dropped.

"Razor!" Zora called out. "I forgot about him. We need to get over there and help him before it's too late."

"I thought he died," Gorva added. "But I wasn't going to say anything until we were free."

Razor lifted him thumb in the air. "I'm not dead yet, gorgeous."

Gorva whispered to Zora, "I don't think I would miss him."

"I heard that!" Razor said. "They say when you're dying, your senses become supersensitive. I must be dying. Does anyone else hear that rattling sound?"

"No," Jakoby said. The drizzle turned to large drops of steady rain. He opened his mouth and caught them on his tongue. "Wet your tongue, Razor."

Razor didn't respond.

"He's out again." Zora heard a distant rattle and bent her ear in the direction of the sound. "I think I hear rattling."

"It's better than hearing goblin war drums." Jakoby

stretched his neck. "Down the road, I see something moving."

Everyone started to rise.

"It's a wagon!" Gorva said. She called out, "Over here —*oof!*"

Zora elbowed the orcen woman. "Will you be silent? We don't know if it's an enemy or not. We need to scoot down to the riverbank, out of sight, until we know who we're dealing with."

"Agreed," Jakoby said. "I'm not sure why anyone would ride down to this spot. There's nothing here but the view. Scoot, everyone, down into that grass."

"That person might be friendly," Gorva argued.

"Or a scavenger who will cut our throats. Do you want to take that chance?" Jakoby asked.

"No."

"Then, scoot!" he said.

"Easier said than done," Zora replied.

Somehow the group scooted, twisted, and rolled over the rise to the sandy beach of the riverbank.

"I'm on bottom again," Zora said with Jakoby half sitting on her head. "Do you mind?"

"Sorry, I thought you were a rock." He lifted up and sat back down. "Is that better?"

"It will be once I get the smell of your trousers out of my hair," Zora said.

"Everyone, be silent," Gorva warned. "I can hear something."

"Now she wants to be quiet," Zora murmured.

They heard a rickety wagon approaching from the west. The rattling of metal came to an end as it stopped. The rain began to pour down.

Zora tried to rise and see over the top of the bank. She squirmed until she could move more freely. "Try to push me up higher."

Jakoby and Gorva shifted her up to the top of the tangled pile of bodies.

"What do you see?" Gorva asked.

"I see a horse-drawn wagon, no driver." Out of the corner of her eye, she caught sight of a person fast approaching with a sword out. It was a burly figure in a hooded traveler's cloak. "They saw us," she said. "Get me down!"

"Don't move," the man said. He held the sword's tip in front of her eyes. "I'd hate to accidentally poke one of those beautiful green eyes out... Zora."

She looked up and gazed into a warm smiling face. "Crane!"

13

"SWEET GAPOLI, look what you got yourself into," Crane said, a surprised look on his portly face. The paunchy man slid down the bank, tripped, and fell at the bottom, crashing face-first into the sandy bank. He rolled onto his side, lay casually on the ground, and spit sand from his mouth. "So much for a rescue."

"Crane, can you get us out of this mess?" Zora pleaded.

"Give me a moment. I'm working on it." He propped himself on one knee, dusted off his purple robes, stood, and shook all over. His belly jiggled. He grabbed it and said, "Ho! Ho! Ho!"

Talon exchanged curious glances.

"Who is this jester?" Gorva asked.

"A friend," Zora added.

Crane inspected the chains and ropes and rubbed his

jaw. He tugged on them, and the bonds tightened.

"Don't do that, you fool," Gorva said.

"Take it easy, beautiful. I know what I'm doing." He offered her a winning smile, and with a twinkle in his eye, he said, "My name's Crane. What's yours?"

Gorva bared her teeth and glared at him.

"You know, you're even more gorgeous when you do that. Perhaps I should keep some of these chains around for later."

"Crane, behave yourself!" Zora said. "Get us out of these knots."

"All right, all right, I'm working on it." He grabbed a length of chain and closed his eyes. "These chains and ropes are enchanted with an entanglement spell. It's no wonder you can't get out."

"What do we do?" Jakoby asked.

"Ah, my dear friend, don't you fret. I have just the thing." Crane rummaged through his robes with his chubby hands. He revealed a ring of many keys and rattled them. "I can open just about anything with these. I traded a filipine jailer for them. A steep price, and you know what? This is the first time I've ever had to use them."

"Why don't you use them, then, and stop talking?" Gorva suggested.

"Patience. I still have to find the right key." He fished through the keys one by one, stopped, and held Zora's wrist cuffs in his hand. "Interesting, they don't have a keyhole."

She rolled her eyes. "They used the pins, Crane. You have to remove the pins."

He tilted his head. "Oh, sounds like we have a problem."

Jakoby leaned his head back and sighed.

"No worries, my friend, no worries." Crane bit his tongue as he worked. "That filipine jailer assured me these keys would work on any shackle." He went through key after key after key. "Not this one. Not that one. Oh my, that one is pretty. I bet it can open a jewelry box. Ah-ha!"

One of the keys was nothing more than a straight metal pin.

"Let me see that cuff," Crane said. He eyed the tiniest pinhole that linked the cuffs together. He jammed the key into the pinhole.

The chains constricted like a living snake and pulled the group into a tight knot.

Zora choked from a coil of rope that twisted around her neck. "Crane, you're killing us!"

"I almost have it. Hang on," he said as he pushed his key in deeper.

The ropes snaked around the others' necks and constricted.

Zora tugged at the cord wrapped around her neck. She couldn't breathe. Jakoby's and Gorva's eyes bulged in their sockets. Leena had her eyes squeezed shut.

I'm going to die! Zora thought.

Pop!

The ropes loosened. The shackles fell from her ankles and wrists.

Everyone but Crane fell to the ground, gasping for air.

"There you go!" Crane said proudly. He twirled the key ring on his finger, and it vanished into thin air. He helped Zora up and patted her on the back. "You'll be fine. You're a strong girl."

She rubbed her raw throat. "Those chains were alive. They were going to kill us."

Like slithering snakes, the chains and ropes slithered toward the river water.

"They would have killed you eventually. That's what they do. An evil magic." Crane offered his hand to Gorva. "Here, let me help you up."

"No thank you!" Gorva picked up a large rock, chased down the chains, and started beating them with it. "Die, devilish thing!"

"I'd stay away from them. They'll wrap you up again!" Crane hollered. He nudged Zora. "I'd rather save that privilege for myself."

"It's a wicked device. It needs to be destroyed!" Gorva bashed one of the cuffs with a stone. "How do we kill it?"

"Leave it alone. The spell will wear off eventually."

The chains retreated to the river and vanished into the rushing deep.

"Those Doom Riders are craftier than I suspected," he said.

Zora's nape hairs rose. "How did you know they were Doom Riders?"

Jakoby and Leena crowded Crane.

Jakoby grabbed the older man by his robes and lifted him onto his toes. "How did you know that?"

"What's with the hostility? Of course I knew it was the Doom Riders. First, gourn tracks are easily defined, and second, we've been searching for you."

"We've?" Zora pinched Crane's chubby face in her hand. "We who?"

Crane started to talk, but his words came out garbled.

Jakoby shook the lesser man. "Answer her!"

"I'm trying," Crane muttered. "Let me explain, please."

Zora dropped her hand. "Make it quick, Crane. We're all out of patience."

He gave her a hurt look. "Boy, you sure have a funny way of showing gratitude. Remember, I'm the one who saved you?"

Jakoby shook him. "Who are you with?"

Crane became defiant. "I'm with Anya. That's who!"

Zora's heart skipped, and her fingers tingled. "But Anya's dead."

"No," Crane said, his warm smile returning. "She's just as alive as you and me."

14

"WHERE IS SHE? WHERE IS SHE?" Zora shouted.

Crane slid his gaze up to Jakoby. "If the dark knight would be so kind as to release me, I'd be happy to explain."

Zora nodded at Jakoby, who let go of Crane and said, "The dark knight. I like it."

Crane adjusted his robes, which were well-worn and frayed around the hem. Zora had spent a lot of time with Crane when he'd taken her to Dark Mountain. His clothing had been impeccable and his boots polished, but now he had a disheveled look, and his soft eyes were tired and showing deeper crow's feet. Plus, all of his garish jewelry was gone.

She gave him a big hug. "I'm sorry, Crane. Thank you for saving us."

"Now, that's more like." He held her tight and lifted her

to her toes. "You know I wouldn't let anything happen to you. Anyway, Anya, Cinder, and Streak went after the boys, and I came after you."

"Cinder and Streak are together?"

"Father and son reunited," he replied.

"But how did you know where to find us?" she asked.

"So many questions, so little faith. Do you remember the Medallion of Location? I still have the jewel box that tracks it down. The medallion has been in Grey Cloak's possession all these years, though we lost him for a decade," Crane said. "Anyway, we were closing in, hiding if you will, when we saw the Doom Riders heading north with the boys in tow. We noticed all the extra horses and gear, so I backtracked, and Anya went after the boys."

"What were you waiting for? Why didn't you attack them when you had the chance?" Jakoby demanded.

"It's not that simple. Anya is the last Sky Rider. They can't take any risk of drawing attention to themselves and being seen. She said she would make her move when the time was right, and even then, they would only have a sliver of a chance." Crane took Zora by the hand and towed her up the riverbank. "Come and say hi to Vixen. She's missed you."

"Where's Leena?" Gorva suddenly asked.

Zora's head snapped up. "Dragon dung, we forgot about Razor!" She pulled Crane up the hill.

Leena was sitting on the hillside, holding Razor's head

in her lap. Her eyes were closed, and her palms covered his face as she mumbled. Razor's tanned skin had turned white.

Zora knelt beside Razor and held his hand. She looked up at the others. "He's so cold." She sniffed. "He's dead."

With his head down, Jakoby recalled, "Dalsay said that not all of us would make it out of Thannis."

"But he didn't go into Thannis." Zora sobbed.

"There, there, perhaps he isn't all the way dead," Crane said as he squatted beside her. He produced a fancy wine bottle made out of purple glass that shined like metal with gold netting all over it. He twisted off the cap. "I've been saving this for a long time. I had a feeling that one of you was going to need it."

Zora wiped the tears from her eyes. "He's dead. Certainly that can't bring back the dead."

Leena shook her head and placed her hand on Razor's heart. She tapped her hand like a heartbeat.

"He's still alive?" Zora asked.

"It's only hard to tell because he's not talking," Jakoby said with a grin.

Crane poured a translucent purple liquid into Razor's mouth. "We need to roll him on his side and pull those bolts out. When we do, I need to pour this over the wounds. Get his tunic off."

They stripped Razor down to the waist. His entire frame was corded in knots of solid muscle. They pulled the bolts out one by one and poured liquid into each wound on both sides. Razor moaned in pain.

"Is he going to live?" Zora asked.

"Live? I don't know. It's up to him, but he shouldn't be bleeding anymore. Let's get him in the wagon." Crane capped the bottle. "Load up, everyone. It's time to roll."

Zora sat beside Crane on the front bench of the wagon with the wind racing through her hair. Vixen, a beautiful mare with a shiny black coat, thundered down the road, pulling the wagon and all its passengers with ease.

"What do you see?" Crane asked Zora.

In the palm of her hands, she held a golden gem-encrusted jewelry box. The lid was open, and a velvety-black sky hovered inside with a silvery ring in the middle. A bright-green dot at the top of the box slowly moved toward the center. "The dot's near the edge but slowly moving."

"Yes, that's good. They are leagues ahead and have a day on us, but they're moving slowly." He pointed at the northern sky. "Those winter clouds coming from the north will slow them down and give us time to catch them."

"Then what?"

"With any luck, Anya will have taken care of the 'then what?' She's quite a gal, that one."

"Is she well?"

The corner of Crane's mouth turned into a smile. "Oh,

she's well all right." He bumped shoulders. "But not as well as you."

"You big flatterer."

"Flattery will get you everywhere." He looked over his shoulder. "Now tell me about your gorgeous friend Gorva. What sanctuary of angels did you find her in?"

The green dot inside the jewelry box vanished.

"Uh, Crane, the green dot is gone," she said.

"Gone!" He gave her the reins and looked inside the box. He shook the box. "This happens sometimes. Here, you hold it."

He exchanged the box for the reins again, pulled out his horsewhip, and yelled to his passengers in the back, "Grab ahold of something, everyone!" He flicked the whip, and the lash sparked. The wheels caught fire, and the horse's shoes burned with flame. "Roll, Wheels of Fire! Roll!"

Vixen sped up so fast that Zora fell back into the laps of the others.

Gorva's eyes were as big as saucers. "The wagon is on fire! The horse is a demon!"

"The horse isn't a demon!" Crane hollered. "She's a speed demon!"

15

"OVER HERE, OVER HERE!" Jakoby hollered above the sound of the pouring rain. The former Monarch Knight was waving his arm overhead. He pointed at the ground. "It's a Doom Rider."

Zora and company had caught the trail of the Doom Riders and even found their horses grazing in the fields less than a league away. All of their gear that was taken was still intact. He hurried over to Jakoby.

The Doom Rider named Scar lay in the mud, dead as a stone. His open eyes looked skyward.

"There was a battle here. A great one," Jakoby said.

"I found another one!" Gorva called out from nearby.

"Dead or alive?" Jakoby hollered.

Gorva tilted her head. "Oh, it's dead. Burned alive, and

headless. Good work. By the looks of it, I think it's the one with the leg that Razor cut off."

They found Shamrok as well. The redheaded Doom Rider had a fatal chest wound.

"That's all of them except for Drysis," Zora said as her gaze swept the hills. "We need to find her."

"We should split up," Jakoby suggested.

"No, we're sticking together. We can't take any chances. For all we know, more might be lurking in those hills," Zora said.

Jakoby laid a hand on her shoulder. "Well said, Zora. You have a knack for taking charge. Perhaps you should become a Monarch Knight someday."

She gave him a funny look. "I don't know about that."

"Hey!" Crane said. "I think the little chatterbox might have found something."

Leena had moved west away from the party and through a path of crushed grass.

Zora shrugged. "Get the horses and gear. Let's follow her."

A quarter of a league away, the company, led by Leena, caught sight of a lone gourn standing in the middle of a field. It lifted its head and set its eyes on the approaching group. It reared up, clawing the air, and let out an earsplitting whinny.

Jakoby sneered. "I don't know which is worse, those dragon horses or their passengers."

"Do you smell that?" Gorva asked.

Zora's nose crinkled. The scent of brimstone lingered in the air. "I do." She could see a circle in the grass that had burned. "It looks like a dragon turned something into ashes." She looked at Jakoby. "Do you think it's Drysis?"

He nodded. "They say the gourn will stay with their masters long after they're dead. They are loyal hounds."

"We need to be sure," Zora said.

Jakoby nodded. He drew the sword he'd recovered from the Ruins of Thannis out of the gear on the horses.

Gorva joined him with a spear.

Leena appeared between them with her nunchakus in hand.

Zora was sitting in the wagon with Crane, and she heard him utter, "I'm not much of a fighter. Lover, yes. Fighter, no. Did I mention I'm a great lover?"

"You've said it a few dozen times before."

Crane gave his usual look of surprise in which his mouth opened in the shape of an *O*. "Good. Those are words for you to remember me by. The first part anyway."

Jakoby, Leena, and Gorva spread out and surrounded the gourn.

The scaly beast huffed out a plume of flames. Its nostrils smoked.

Jakoby held his free hand out and inched closer to the beast. "Easy, fella, we only want to get a closer look."

The gourn lowered the curled horns on its head. Its front claws raked the muddy dirt.

"I can see a body!" Jakoby said. "Or what is left of one! It's only charred remains!" He glanced at the gourn. "Easy, fella. I'm backing away." He glanced down at the heap of bones and ashes. "It's her!"

"How do you know?" Zora hollered back.

His smile showed his white teeth. "I can see her crossbow. No mistaking the shape. It's like a cross—or what's left of one. Little more than twigs now!"

"You know, gourn are neutral beasts," Crane stated. "We could tame one. It would be very valuable, but a new master needs to break him."

"Are you suggesting I try to ride that thing?" Jakoby asked.

Crane leaned forward. "No, I'm suggesting you break all of them. It's either that or they try to kill us." He poked his chubby finger outward. "It has brothers."

Two gourn appeared in the high grass. They sauntered toward the group, breathing fire.

"This might be a problem," Crane muttered.

"Might be?" asked Zora, exasperated. "They're dragons, aren't they? Without wings?"

Crane shrugged. "I'm no expert, but they look like dragons and breathe fire like dragons." He cupped his hands over his mouth. "Jakoby! Try to ride one! They can be broken."

"I'm not getting on that thing!"

"Then you're going to have to kill it!" Crane said.

Jakoby shook his head and brandished his sword. He ran the blade over the palm of his hand. "You're a fine blade. Serve me well."

Gorva lowered her spear and crouched. She spit on the ground. "I'll kill a beast myself!"

Leena moved toward the third gourn, whirling her nunchakus, spinning them like wildfire.

Zora grabbed Crane's arm and squeezed. "We have to help them."

"I will." He closed his eyes. "I'm going to pray."

16

JAKOBY, Leena, and Gorva faced off with the gourn.

The dragon beasts wandered forward with their horns low to the ground. The fire from their breath licked up the wet grass, creating a fog-like steam.

Zora sat in the wagon with her stomach in knots. "The gourn are huge. They'll run them over. We have to do something." She elbowed Crane. "Stop praying and do something!"

Crane kept his fingers locked with his index fingers creating a steeple. His eyes were squeezed shut as he prayed silently in the pouring rain.

The gourn charged.

"Goy!" Zora jumped into the back of the wagon and started rummaging through her gear.

As much faith as she had in her friends, they didn't

appear to be a match for the gourn. The dragons were bigger than horses, with hides like scale armor, and they breathed dragon flame.

She found a small rucksack she carried and spread open the neck. She plunged her hand inside.

"What are you looking for, darling?" Razor asked. His eyes were open, and he lay flat on his back. "Perhaps I can help."

She shook her head. "Where is it? Where is it? Where is it?" She dumped the contents of the pack into the bed of the wagon.

Razor tilted his head. His fingers wrapped around an object in sackcloth. "I found something. Is it a rock you're looking for?"

Zora set her gaze on his fist. "Give me that."

"Give me a kiss first."

"It sounds like you're feeling better." She grabbed his hand. "But I don't have time to play games."

"Ah, come on. One little kiss won't hurt anyone."

"Have you no shame? Give me the stone, or our friends will die!"

"Only if you don't kiss me." Razor puckered up.

"Fine!" She kissed his lips. "Can I have the stone now?"

He gave her a dreamy smile. "You can have anything you want, doll."

"Ugh!" She took the sackcloth from his hand and freed the stone from it. The dragon charm glowed in her palm.

She jumped out of the wagon and raced toward the others.

Crane twisted around in his seat and said to Razor, "That was smooth, but Zora's mine, and Gorva. You can have the quiet one."

Razor pulled himself over the lip of the wagon bed. His eyes locked on Zora. "She kissed me first. That means she's mine."

"Fine, but Gorva is all mine. Hands off."

Razor nodded. "Fair enough."

"Stop! Stop!" Zora shouted. She carried the dragon charm high over her head. She didn't understand how the eyeball-shaped gemstone worked, but she'd used it before. "Stop!"

Gorva stabbed at a gourn, keeping it at bay.

Leena had hopped onto a gourn's back and was riding it like a bronco. She clubbed it with her nunchakus, and it bucked her free of its back.

Jakoby's sword bit into the horns of his attacker. It knocked Jakoby off his feet with a swing of its bull neck. Flames blasted out of its mouth. Jakoby jumped away in the nick of time before he was turned into a campfire.

Without thinking, Zora sped in front of the gourn bearing down on Jakoby. She held the gleaming blue charm out before her and yelled, "Stop!" once more.

The beast skidded to a halt. The flames in its eyes cooled, and it sat down in the grass.

Zora's heart raced as she stood in the soaking rain and watched the other two gourn approach. "Sit," she said through gritted teeth.

The pair of gourn sat like dogs beside the first, three in a row. Their eyes were fastened on the twinkling charm.

Zora was so close, she could feel their hot breath on her face. She stepped closer.

"Be careful," Jakoby warned.

She placed her hand on the middle gourn's nose. "It's okay."

Even sitting down, the gourn was a head taller than the half-elf woman.

"Get on the backs of those things, and ride 'em!" Crane hollered.

Razor had joined the older man on the wagon's bench. He was slouched over and holding his side. "Ride that drag-on!" He doubled over. "Oooch."

"You heard Crane," Zora said to Jakoby. "Get on."

"What?" Jakoby touched his chest. "Me? I'm not getting on that thing. Why don't you send them away? I don't want anything to do with them."

"I thought Monarch Knights could ride four-footed

beasts," Gorva said. She approached the gourn she'd battled with. "I've ridden dragons. My father, Hogrim, was a Sky Rider. These gourn aren't so different." She climbed into the saddle.

The gourn rose to all fours. It vaulted into a gallop and started to buck. Gorva held on. The dragon beast calmed, rolled its neck, and trotted around the others.

"Anything she can do," Jakoby said as he mounted the gourn, "I can do as well."

His gourn lurched up and charged into a full gallop. It pitched and bucked like a wild mule.

Jakoby let out a shout. "Yeeee-hah!"

Zora smiled. Her friends had their beasts under control. Even Leena started to ride. Zora rubbed the dragon charm in the palm of her hand. It was warm, like a living thing. She could feel a connection to the gourn. Their strength seemed to flow into her.

I don't know how I'm doing this, but I am. I like it!

For years, she'd roamed Gapoli with Talon, searching for dragon charms. When they'd found them, Dalsay had been quick to take them away, but she had always wished to have one. Now she did, and it was one of the most amazing things she'd ever felt. She kissed it and tucked it back inside her pocket.

Maybe there's more to me after all.

Zora met Crane and Razor at the wagon.

"Good job, gal," Razor said.

"Great job!" Crane offered a hand and helped her into the wagon. "Well done, Zora. You are much, much more than meets the eye, and that's saying a lot."

"Perhaps your prayers were answered," she said as she scooted in between them.

"I have no doubt there are angels among us." Crane watched the others race through the rain on the backs of the gourn.

Even Leena smiled.

Crane flicked the reins. "Onward, Vixen. Ride with the storm."

"We're staying with the rain?" Zora asked.

"There are eyes in the sky. The rain is the best way to avoid them. I have a feeling that's what Anya did."

"Do you know where they went?" Zora asked.

Crane tapped his nose. "The Brotherhood of Whispers is the keeper of many secrets." He leaned into her. "And the less you know, the better."

"How much farther?" Grey Cloak yelled.

Streak shrugged. "I don't know. I'm following them."

"Great." Grey Cloak lowered his body and hugged the dragon's back. His teeth clattered together. "I really miss my cloak now."

Ahead, Cinder and Anya raced through the icy-cold storm clouds, where lightning flashed and brightened the sky. Dyphestive lay in Cinder's saddle bundled up in the Cloak of Legends. The strapping blond was in the worst shape Grey Cloak had ever seen him.

Be well, Dyphestive. Be well.

Grey Cloak's fingers and toes were numb and as frozen as icicles. Streak's dips and turns didn't help either. The sky-riding maneuvers turned his stomach over and again. He couldn't get used to it, and he dry heaved several times as a result. The only saving grace was the warmth that Streak's body provided. It kept him from turning entirely to ice.

I hope this ends soon. At least Dyphestive isn't awake for it. He smirked. *Who am I kidding? He'd probably enjoy it.*

The worse the conditions, the more Dyphestive thrived. The youth had always been a glutton for punishment. Rhonna had worked him like a plow horse at her farm, and never once had Dyphestive complained about it. The more she gave him, the harder he worked, even with the most menial tasks, from shoveling manure to sweeping cobwebs out of the barns. Never once did Dyphestive whine about it.

On the other hand, Grey Cloak had put effort into cutting corners and finishing the job quicker. He had never been a fan of backbreaking work, not that anyone would be. But Rhonna, a proven taskmaster, had kept him on his toes from dawn to dusk. It had made him tough, and during times like this, he needed to be.

"Why don't you try to sleep?" Streak suggested.

"I don't sleep much," he replied as he nuzzled the softer fleshy ridges between Streak's neck and back. "I'm fine."

"Suit yourself, but I don't have any idea how long this flight will be. Flying in the cover of clouds is a lot slower than using the air streams," Streak said.

"We'll get there when we get there." Grey Cloak yawned. As uncomfortable as he was, he laid his head down. Wedged safely between the dragon's wings, he dozed off.

A bumpy ride woke Grey Cloak. His body bounced on the dragon's back. His fingers found a grip before he slipped off. He wiped the drool from his mouth and raised his head. It was pitch-black, and the harsh winds roared past his ears.

"What's going on?" he asked.

"We're getting ready to dive," Streak said.

"Dive where?"

"We're circling in the clouds above Lake Flugen. Cinder is making sure the way is clear."

Grey Cloak nodded. "All right."

Cinder rose up beside them. His great wings were stretched out, and the two dragons glided side by side. He turned his head in their direction. "The way is clear of those nasty flying lizards. Follow me into the lake, and don't delay."

Streak nodded. "Will do, Father."

Grey Cloak caught Anya looking at him. Her damp hair streaked behind her head. She rested one of her hands on Dyphestive's broad back.

"How's he doing?" he yelled.

She offered a sad look and shrugged.

Cinder dove. His tremendous body dropped, creating a pinwheel of clouds behind him, and vanished.

"Hang on!" Streak said.

"Wait," Grey Cloak said, aghast. "Did he say *into* Lake Flugen?"

"Why do you think I said hang on?" Streak replied coyly. "Oh, and don't forget to hold your breath." He dove.

Grey Cloak felt his stomach move up into his throat. He locked his fingers onto a dragon horn and hung on for dear life.

As soon as they cleared the stormy clouds and plunged into the lower altitude, he was smothered in warm southern air. He basked in the warmth.

Ah, this is better.

Smothered in the darkness of night, he scanned the horizon. Out of the corner of his eye, he caught sight of Gunder Island in the distance. He could see the shoreline, too, but they were diving fast. He looked down. Lake Flugen's black waters were rushing up to greet them.

He let out a scream. "Aaaaaaaaaaahhhhh!"

"Hold your breath, master!" Streak said.

Grey Cloak took a quick breath and hunkered down on the dragon's back. They crashed into the waters and plunged deep into the inky depths.

As if I wasn't wet enough already. He opened his eyes, but he couldn't see a thing. *I really could use the Cloak of Legends right now.*

It was in those very waters where the Cloak of Legends imbued him with the power to swim, breathe, and see underwater like a fish. This time, however, the experience was entirely different. Streak's swim was long. Grey Cloak's lungs began to burn, and Streak swam deeper still. Grey Cloak's eyes felt like they were going to pop. His entire life was a watery blur. He was trapped.

Hurry, Streak, hurry! I'm going to suffocate!

18

THE NEXT THING Grey Cloak remembered was him lying on a shore, spitting up water. Something firmly patted his back. He turned his head as he wiped his mouth and looked at Streak, who showed worry in his bright-yellow eyes.

"Are you okay, dude?" Streak asked.

Grey Cloak coughed a few times. "I've never felt better after nearly drowning. Where are we anyway?"

Streak shrugged his wings. "Beats me."

Anya stood on the sandy beach with Cinder behind her and Dyphestive lying nearby.

"This is Safe Haven." She wrung the water from her wavy locks.

"It reminds me of Thannis." He spied the stalactites hanging in the massive cavern's high ceiling. Emerald stones glowed in the dripping rock formations, creating an eerie illumination. He noticed shells on the shoreline that stretched in both directions for half a league and ended in blackness. "Please tell me this isn't another city of undead."

"No, it's Safe Haven. Why would it be filled with the dead?" She hooked him underneath his arms and lifted him to his feet. "Safe Haven, you can relax."

Grey Cloak brushed the sand off of his arms. "So, this is your hideout, eh?"

She nodded. "It's the best-kept secret in Gapoli. If not for Safe Haven, we'd have been killed a decade ago."

"We? As in you and Cinder? Here all that time, all alone?"

Cinder barked out a dragon call that was directed toward the caves in the back of the cavern.

Grey Cloak covered his ears. "Thanks for the warning. What was that?"

"Cinder is calling for aid. Dyphestive isn't out of the woods yet," she said.

Grey Cloak sat down by his brother and studied his peaked face. "He looks awful." He took Dyphestive's hand. "He's cold. Be strong, brother."

Streak lay down beside Dyphestive as well and nuzzled up against him. "I'll keep the big fella warm."

Grey Cloak stood up. "How do you survive down here? What do you eat? Fish?"

Anya shook her hair and combed her fingers through it.

Cinder swung his neck around and breathed out a blast of hot air. Her sun-bleached locks had darkened to auburn, but she was dry from head to toe. She tied her hair into a ponytail. "Yes, we eat a lot of fish. We eat whatever we can to survive."

"So, how long is it going to be before help arrives?"

"It won't be long, but we might as well make a fire." She started gathering driftwood. "Have you ever heard of the Shelf?" she asked.

"Yes, of course."

"Well, Safe Haven is linked to the Shelf. It's a long and treacherous journey between the two, but it's the perfect spot for hiding." She dropped the driftwood on a spot near Dyphestive that Grey Cloak had cleared. "But it's extremely difficult to get here."

"How did you find it?"

"I've always known. My uncle, Justus, brought me here when I first became a Sky Rider. He told me to come here if the dangers were ever too grave, and we would reunite." She frowned. "But that's not possible now. I miss them."

Grey Cloak nodded. "I wish I'd taken the time to get to know them better."

"No time for regrets. As much as I hate to admit it, they were wrong to try to quarantine you for life. They paid the ultimate price for it." She patted Streak on his flat skull and eyed the pile of wood. "Do you mind?"

Streak spit a small ball of flame at the driftwood, setting it ablaze. "Enjoy."

The dry wood popped and crackled.

Grey Cloak hunkered down by the wood, rubbed his hands together, and enjoyed the warmth on his frozen toes. For the longest time, the group sat in silence. It gave him time to reflect on the battle with the Doom Riders. They'd won. He had the figurine, but at what cost?

His gaze fell on his brother. *Lord of Light, please make him well.* He cleared his throat. "So, how did you find us?"

"We don't stay in here all of the time and live like hermits." She smoothed her ponytail over her shoulder. "I've kept in close contact with Crane."

"You have?"

She nodded. "He said you reappeared."

He tilted his head. "Reappeared? Zooks!" He snapped his fingers. "The Medallion of Location! Forgive me, brother." He rummaged through the Cloak of Legend's inner pocket and produced the Medallion of Location. It was a large golden coin inlaid with tiny jewels in an arcane pattern. He dropped on his backside. "Whoa."

Anya stirred the fire with a small stick. "I hate to admit it, but after ten years, we were losing hope. But Crane said he checked the locater box every day, and you popped up. We didn't waste any time tracking you down after we rendezvoused. Cinder and I came after you. Crane went after the other members of Talon. They should be safe now."

Grey Cloak rolled the coin over his slender fingers. "That's fantastic news. It appears that I'm not as lost as I thought I was after all."

"So, where have you been the last decade?" she asked.

Even Cinder moved closer and turn his head to listen.

"You might find it hard to believe, but I haven't"—he glanced at Dyphestive—"or we haven't been anywhere, exactly. We entered the Wizard Watch, battled the underlings that I summoned, and we ran for our lives through the Time Mural. We ended up being ten years in the future, if that makes any sense."

"It doesn't," she said. "What are underlings?"

"Evil beings from another world that I accidentally summoned when I used the Figurine of Heroes to get us out of trouble. It backfires sometimes. I should have listened to Tatiana and never used it."

Anya's beautiful face darkened. "Tatiana. I warned you she was trouble."

19

"TATIANA ISN'T SO BAD, I've learned," Grey Cloak said. "She risked her life to save us. If not for her, we'd be dead."

Anya raised her eyebrows. "She died?"

"No, she's alive, at least according to Dalsay." Grey Cloak brought Anya up to speed about his relationship between Tatiana and the spirit of Dalsay. "They give us eyes and ears in the tower. As long as they are alive, we have knowledge of what the Wizard Watch are doing. If we're going to defeat Black Frost, we're going to need to take the Wizard Watch down as well."

"The Wizard Watch in the east is guarded by an army. That includes the elves, the Black Guard, and Riskers. It's going to be impossible to get in there," she said.

"I'll think of something." He spoke about his journey into the future, how he'd almost died, but Dyphestive had saved him. He explained how they'd met the gnome, Chopper, and the cyclops, Tiny. He told her that Rhonna had been made the leader of Dwarf Skull. "We have allies. We can win this."

"No, we have to win this." Anya stood up and paced. "Over the past ten years, Black Frost's strength in numbers has only grown. The Riskers and Black Guard rule every major city in all nine territories. Any who oppose him die a quick death." Her hand fell to the pommel of her Sky Blade. "Yet, many embrace Black Frost and worship him like a god. The Monarchs revel in his conquests." She sneered. "They are complicit. It disgusts me. I thought they were good men and women, but their hearts were rotten. The Monarchs are supposed to fight this evil no matter the cost."

"I'm not making excuses, but it sounds to me like they've chosen safety over liberty. That's just no way to live," Grey Cloak said. "It disgusts me as well. Black Frost has them all fooled. But their hearts will change once all of their freedom is gone. We can only hope it's not too late."

"We'll get them, boss," Streak said with his twin tails drumming behind him.

Grey Cloak looked at his dragon. "Speaking of changes, what happened to you exactly? You went from a runt to a middling in about a week."

Streak's pink tongue flickered out of his mouth. "Shortly after we left Prisoner's Island, my tummy started rumbling, and I let out a belch that scattered the sea birds. I grew tired, nestled in the marshes, and slept. I woke inside a warm and gooey cocoon with strands of stickiness all around me. I busted out of the weird egg, starving to death, and I devoured an entire crocodile. That's when I discovered I was as big as a horse." Streak opened his big jaws and yawned. "I still had a sense of where you'd gone and headed south. That's when I came across Anya and Cinder."

"I'm glad you're back. I'm glad you all are. We only need to get Dyphestive back," he said.

"Perhaps I can help with that." It was a familiar voice.

Everyone turned their heads and fastened their stares on the hermit Than. The hermit wore a set of tattered robes, and his long red-gray hair was in tangles. He was still tall but was stooped over and carried a gnarled wooden walking stick. His facial features were strong, and there was a warm brightness in his gold-flecked eyes, but his jaw sagged. The scaly skin on his arms looked like a shedding snake's. His fingernails were long.

"Forgive my appearance. The last decade hasn't been good to me. My gorgeous hair dries out, and my skin ages like a mummy. Black Frost's power grows, and mine weakens," Than said in a scratchy voice.

Grey Cloak felt compelled to rise. "Nevertheless, it's good to see you, Than. I believe we've all changed."

Than pinched his cheek. "Says the elf with skin as tight

as the head of a drum." He took a knee beside Dyphestive and handed Grey Cloak his cane. "And stop calling me Than."

"Of course, Thanadiliditis."

Than swept his hair out of his eyes and over his shoulders. "Don't call me that either. It's an alias."

Grey Cloak looked at Anya, who wasn't looking at him. "Alias for what?"

"Nath. You see, I only swapped the letters around and made the rest of it up. Oh, it's not my full name but the short version. If I said the long version, I'd probably die before I finished."

"I like Nath better," Grey Cloak commented.

"Yes, well, good." Nath cleared this throat and began his inspection of Dyphestive. He peeled the youth's eyelids back. "This is bad."

"How bad?" Grey Cloak asked.

"Look at his eyes. See the yellow that should be white? That's poison." Nath opened up the cloak and looked at the scar on Dyphestive's chest. "Gads. He was shot in the heart, and he still breathes?"

Grey Cloak nodded. "He's stubborn."

"Heh, he's either as lucky as a leprechaun or extremely gifted. Hmm..." Nath scratched the scraggly hairs on his cheek with his yellow fingernails. "I can help him. The poison attacks the heart. That's where it does most of the damage. It's fascinating that he's still alive, even with his ability to heal."

"What are you going to do?" Grey Cloak asked.

"I have to destroy the poison, attack it from the inside out." Nath took a breath and closed his eyes. He placed his hand on Dyphestive's broad chest and applied pressure. His hand radiated with golden light. "Here goes."

20

DYPHESTIVE'S CHEST rose and fell, and he snored quietly. He'd been asleep for hours and resting well with the Cloak of Legends covering him like a blanket.

Meanwhile, Streak had spent his time swimming in the lake, gathering fish to eat.

Squatting on his legs, Nath stuck a stick in a large bass and placed it over the campfire, where other fish were cooking. "I always enjoyed fishing back home. It gave me peace of mind and taught me patience." He let out a ragged sigh and dropped to his backside. "My knees aren't what they used to be, nor the rest of me for that matter."

"Healing Dyphestive took a lot out of you, didn't it?" Grey Cloak asked.

"As long as I'm using my powers for good, I'll be fine."

"I thank you. I'm sure Dyphestive will be grateful, too,

when he awakens." Grey Cloak grabbed one of the skewered fish that was charred all over its scales. "Let me prepare you something to eat."

"Don't be silly." Nath took the stick and pulled hot fish off the end. "The day I can't feed myself, you might as well shoot me. It probably won't kill me, but shoot me nevertheless." Using the sharp fingernail on his index finger like a knife, he cut the meaty fish open.

Anya was nibbling on her fish, and she started to giggle. "Those are some very sharp fingernails. How long has it been since you cut them?"

Nath clenched and unclenched his scaly fingers. "Funny, I don't think that I've ever cut them, or filed them for the matter. Dragons don't do that."

Grey Cloak gave Anya a puzzled glance. "Than, er, I mean, Nath," he said as he opened his fish up with a knife. "When we first met, you said to me, 'Steal a dragon. Save the world.' What did you mean by that?"

"Did I say that?" Nath asked as he chewed a hunk of flaky fish meat. He scratched his head. "I did, didn't I? Steal a dragon. Save a dragon. I've used many lines."

Grey Cloak nodded. "Are you talking about you?"

"Yes and no. I've been trapped on this world for years, trying to find heroes who can help. I use many phrases to motivate them." Nath sucked food off his fingers. "Not only is my world in danger but your world as well. Black Frost feeds on my world. It strengthens him and takes my power.

I am in danger, the same as the dragons on your world. He seeks to control them all. He does control them, all of them. We can't let that happen. *The one who rules the dragons is the one who rules the world."*

Grey Cloak drank from his waterskin and wiped his mouth. "Are you a dragon, Nath?"

"It should be obvious by now," Nath said. He held up his flabby arms and jiggled them. "What do these look like?"

"I'd rather not say," Grey Cloak said with a smirk.

"They are scales. Look, they cover my body." He lifted up his robes and removed his tattered pants leg. His lower leg was covered in scales like a fish. "Grey Cloak, you saw my lady friend, Selene, in the cathedral at Monarch City. I'm the same as she is."

"Oh," Grey Cloak said, enlightened. "But she had a tail and was far younger and prettier. And she wasn't a dragon."

"No, not at the moment, but she can turn into one. As can I," Nath said. "You doubt me?"

"It's odd," he said.

"Give me another fish!" Nath demanded.

Grey Cloak handed the old hermit another skewer of roasted fish flesh. "Streak, is Nath a dragon? Because if anyone knows a dragon, it's a dragon."

Streak wandered over to Nath and sniffed him all over. Once he'd finished sniffing, he licked Nath's scales. "Smells like a dragon and tastes like a dragon. He's a dragon."

Grey Cloak set his gaze on Anya. "Is it true? This man is a dragon?"

She nodded.

Grey Cloak stiffened. "Well, why didn't you say something earlier?"

"I like watching you figure things out for yourself. It's amusing." She bit into a hunk of fish and started chewing.

"So, all three of you have been hiding down here all this time?" Grey Cloak asked.

"Us and the fledglings. We've been training them all of these years." Anya picked her teeth and spit out a scale. "I hate it when that happens."

"Dragons?" Streak asked. "What dragons?"

Anya managed a coy smile. "Your brothers and sisters. The fledglings. They are all grown up now."

Streak's tails drummed the beach. He looked up at his father, Cinder. "I want to see them. I want to see them now!"

Cinder nodded. "Come on, son. It's time for a family reunion." He led Streak into the depths of the cavern, and together they vanished into the inky darkness.

"I can't believe so much has happened since I've been gone," Grey Cloak said as he wiped a strand of hair from his eye. "All twelve fledglings are fully grown?"

"Mostly," Anya said as she stood up and dusted her bottom off. "Wait until you see them. Nath has done wonders with them."

Nath smiled, offering a mouthful of perfectly white teeth. "We are all brothers and sisters after all, but they are eager to stretch their wings."

"Whoa, you aren't thinking about taking them outside, are you? It's too risky," Grey Cloak said.

"We're going to build a new army of Sky Riders," Anya said. "We have as many dragons now as the Sky Riders had in Gunder Mountain. More so."

Grey Cloak shook his head. "Anya, you can't think you stand a chance against Black Frost with little more than a baker's dozen Sky Riders. You'll be wiped out, again!"

She narrowed her eyes. "We will see it through, no matter what it takes."

"You're as crazy as your uncle. That line of reasoning got them all killed."

"That's why we have to act quicker than he did," she said.

"You're mad. All of the Sky Riders are obsessed."

Anya stood toe to toe with him and gave him a hard look. "Watch your tongue, elf."

"Say, what's cooking?"

"Stifle it, Dyphestive!"

Grey Cloak and Anya's eyes widened as they simultaneously looked down at Grey Cloak's brother.

"Dyphestive! You're awake!"

21

RED BONE

TALON FOUND shelter from the hard rains in an old barn outside of Red Bone in Sulter Slay's territory. The barn had a leaky roof, and mud puddles formed on the dirt floor. The aged wooden rafters and beams had held up well, but many of the boards on the outside walls were rotten, and the wind whistled through the gaps.

All the horses and gourn and even the wagon were pulled inside the decrepit barn that was void of livestock, but a hive of angry possums thrived and hissed at the invaders.

Gorva poked her spear at the varmints. "Get away, you ugly things! Go! Go!"

"Don't run them off. We might need to eat them," Razor said. He sat up in the back of the wagon, holding his ribs. "Haven't you ever eaten possum? It's delicious."

"No thank you." Gorva chased the possum family into a burrow in the back end of a stall. She pushed an old board over it and set a rock on top. She dusted her hands off. "That's better."

Night had fallen, and all of Talon's members were present except for Crane. He'd gone to visit the cottage of the farmer who he thought owned the land they now occupied.

Zora walked past while Jakoby started a fire in a stone pit. He struck stones together and finally got a fire going in a small bed of dry straw. He added some kindling, and before long, a warm fire burned, illuminating the barn's dreary atmosphere.

Zora rubbed her hands in front of the flames. "We might as well find something to eat."

Leena rummaged through the saddlebags and gathered some rations.

"Blech. More dried rations. I'll pass. Say, are we in Red Bone?" Razor asked in his salty but charming manner. "If that's the case, they have great ale here."

"They have great ale everywhere, according to you," Jakoby commented.

Razor shoved himself off the edge of the wagon. When both feet hit the ground, he grimaced. "Well, they do. I've never been to any town that didn't have good ale to offer."

"Shouldn't you stay off your feet?" Gorva asked.

"Ah, I knew you cared, doll."

"I don't care. I just don't want you getting any closer to me."

Razor offered his palms up in surrender. "I'll be sure to stay away. Besides, Crane placed his claim on you anyway."

Gorva gave him a horrified look. "What? He placed a claim on me?"

Razor cupped his hand to his ear, and with a devilish grin, he said, "I hear those wedding bells ringing."

Everyone broke out in giggles. Even Leena managed a smile that the arachnid tattoo on her face couldn't hide.

The main barn door creaked as it opened a crack. Crane squeezed his rain-soaked, portly body inside. He made a wide-eyed surprised look as he shoved the barn door closed. "Oh, a fire, how nice!" He gave them all a suspicious look. "What? Is there a rat on my head or something?" He glanced upward.

"No, someone special was just talking about you in a very fond way," Razor said as he looked at Gorva.

"Gum up before I rip your tongue out!" Gorva showed Razor her fist.

"Gorva, sweetie," Crane said, "I brought you something." He pulled a cloth away from a loaf of baked bread he'd been carrying. "It's right out of a coal-burning stove, hot and fresh. Have some. Oh, and there's more. I have half a wheel of cheese, and they said they'd be glad to feed us in the morning."

Razor limped across the floor. "I'd be delighted to break bread with you, brother. I'm famished." He took the bread from Crane and tore off a hunk. Steam came out of the middle of the loaf. His nostrils flared. "Ah, that smells good." He ate and talked with his mouth half full.

"Don't be stingy." Jakoby helped himself to the bread and passed it around to the others. The moment he started chewing, his eyes brightened. "That is good."

Crane winked at Gorva. "Don't worry, honey. I don't expect you to be able to bake like this. I'm more concerned about—"

"Don't you dare say it." Gorva glared at him.

"What? I was only going to say I was concerned about your happiness."

"Uh-huh." Gorva started eating the bread. "I wasn't born an orc yesterday."

Zora helped herself to the last piece of bread and nibbled on a hunk of crust. "It's been a long time since I've been through Red Bone. What's changed in the last decade?"

Crane cut off a hunk of the cheese wheel with a knife and tossed it to Zora. "I should have gotten some wine with that cheese. It's good!" He cleared his throat. "Anyway, Sulter Slay remains vastly independent of the cities in the north. Red Bone is a little different, but being so far north in the territory, Dark Mountain's poison has still crept in.

We should be safe here for a while—the farmer assured me."

"You know, we can't trust someone just because they're a farmer," Zora said.

"Yes, you're right, but I vetted him pretty good. He doesn't hold the Black Guard in high regard. He made that clear. The old curmudgeon and his wife both made that perfectly clear. So we should be safe here so long as we avoid the prying eyes of the Black Guard and Riskers."

"Riskers?" Zora almost choked on her bread. "How many Riskers?"

Crane held up both meaty hands. "Easy now."

"Ten!" Gorva said. "Ten Riskers?"

"What?" Crane caught her looking at his spread fingers. "No, not ten." He held up one index finger. "Only one. We can avoid one."

Everyone's shoulders deflated, and they breathed easier.

"How many Black Guards?" Jakoby asked.

"Well, there's significantly more of them. It's a fairly large city." Crane swallowed a lump in his throat and admitted, "A couple hundred or so? That's not too bad, is it?"

"Not unless we do something stupid, like ride into town on a gourn." Zora sighed. "You know, we can't hide the gourn here forever. We have to go somewhere safer. Where did Anya go, and how do we meet up with them again?"

"I'll take care of that," Crane said, "but I'm going to have to go all the way into town to make it happen. Besides, we need to gather more information."

"About what?" Jakoby asked.

Crane eyed him. "About us."

22

ZORA AND CRANE headed into Red Bone early the next afternoon. The outskirts of the city hadn't changed since the last time Zora had passed through them years ago with Talon. It had been her first mission with Grey Cloak and Dyphestive, and they'd stopped for a while to grab supplies. Most of the buildings they passed were barns and storehouses. Farmers worked the wheat fields for miles around.

The heart of Red Bone was a different layout entirely. The buildings were made out of red sandrock that stood three stories tall in some places. The streets were hard-packed dirt and stone, and the rooftops were slightly pitched, almost flat, with slate-gray tiles covering their roofs.

Unlike Raven Cliff, there were no welcoming covered

porches or walkways in front of the buildings. Instead, the doorstops kissed the very roads they traveled on.

Zora fanned herself as they walked down the busy street, where merchants with wagonloads of goods passed them by. The people were ordinary, their clothing durable and weather efficient, and many wore sandals or walked on their bare feet.

"What do you say we get something to eat?" Crane asked as he guided her with his hand on her hip toward a tavern dwelling with its backside to the sun. "It should be cooler in there."

Three horsemen trotted right toward them, cutting off their path to the tavern. They wore red tunics with crests of a black mountain embroidered on the front over chain-mail armor. Their steel helmets were squarish with hard ridges on the top that gleamed in the sunlight. There was no mistaking them. They were the Black Guard.

Crane shoved Zora out of their path and into the wall just as the Black Guard stormed by. "Don't look at them," he whispered. "Don't even glance."

"I know the routine," she replied.

Zora had been dealing with the Black Guard and their devious ways for over ten years. She couldn't get used to their domineering presence. The soldiers of Dark Mountain did as they wished. They were the law, and they let everyone know it.

"Let's get inside."

They entered the open doorway and were greeted by an atmosphere rich in pipe smoke and the smell of greasy meat. In the back of the tavern, a hog roasted over an indoor bed of hot coals. A bald orc with sideburns and meaty, tattooed arms turned the huge hog on a spit while another orc sliced large portions from the beast's cooked meat.

"That's a first," Zora muttered as she navigated her way through a network of small round tables made from storage barrels.

Every bowed floorboard groaned underneath her feet. She made her way to a pair of wooden chairs with spindle backs that sat in the back of the tavern, tucked underneath stairs that led up to the rooms.

She pulled out a chair and sat down. "Is this good for you?"

Crane was at the bar, sitting on a stool, chatting with an attractive halfling bartender who stood on the bar. The halfling had a flirty smile and piles of chestnut hair that matched her eyes. She tugged on Crane's chin and kissed him on the cheek while another human barkeep filled up two tankards of ale. He handed them to Crane, who in turn handed coins over to the halfling lady and kissed both of her cheeks.

The halfling lady waved her little fingers at Zora, and Zora kindly waved back as Crane made his way over with ale sloshing over the rim of his tankards.

"It didn't take you long to make friends, did it?" Zora asked as she took the tankard with both of her hands.

Crane sucked the froth off his ale. "If anyone asks, you're my daughter. I hope you aren't offended."

"Not at all. It's better than the alternative."

"What alternative?"

She kicked her legs up on the table and took a drink. She looked at Crane. "You have froth on your nose."

He wiped the froth off with his finger and sucked it off. "A good man never lets a drop go to waste. I hope you don't mind, but I already ordered us the tavern special."

"Did you ask what it is?"

His eyes fastened on the boar roasting on its spit. "No, but I have a feeling it has pork in it."

Zora nodded. She'd always enjoyed Crane's company. No matter the circumstance, he always maintained the same good, albeit absentminded, mood.

"The ale is good. Razor will be jealous." She scanned the room. "So, what else did you find out during your little chat?"

"We picked the right hovel to come to. Mostly locals who like to chat. They hate the Black Guard and frequent ratholes like this to get away from them."

"Good." Zora scanned the faces in the room. It was mostly an ordinary group of men and women, a mix of most races, hardworking and weathered looking. Their fingernails were dirty, hands callused, and clothing messy.

They smelled of sweat and manure that they'd tracked in from the farms. Many huddled over their tables, talking quietly, swapping gossip, while others played cards or rolled stones. "If there's anything to be heard, this is the place to hear it."

Crane raised his pint. "Let's make some new friends, shall we?"

Zora smiled and raised her tankard. "To new friends who share the same enemy."

23

UNLIKE THE MAJOR cities in the northern territories, the people below the Iron Hills remained set in their ways. Black Guard or no Black Guard, they were going to live life their way. They thrived at working hard, and they enjoyed what they enjoyed. According to them, nothing had changed since the arrival of Dark Mountain's troops.

Of course, that was only talk. The truth was an entirely different matter. The Black Guard had the people of Red Bone underneath their thumb more than their pride would ever let them admit. They served the enemy host reluctantly. Reluctance led to a loss of privileges, prison time, or even death.

"Let's see your cards, young lady," an older man who had a long white scar running up his forearm said.

Zora had joined a group of men playing a game of birds.

They'd been playing for hours, and her pile of silver chips had stacked up. She had five cards in her hand and shuffled the order of the cards around. "Are you sure you want to see them, Judd? The last time I showed them, you didn't fare so well."

"Your luck will run out." Judd eyeballed his cards and licked his lips. "And mine is bound to change."

"Not this again," said an orc with a large belly sitting across from Zora. His name was Moonlar. He tossed his cards down. "I'm down to three silver, so I'm out. Not to mention my wife is going to kill me." He rocked onto the chair's back two legs and lifted a pint. "Ale!" He winked at Zora. "At least I can afford more ale."

The only person at the table was a fish-eyed man named Oyster. He was slight of build with thin hair parted in the middle. He spoke softly, and he studied his cards with piercing eyes. All of the men were older than Zora by a decade or so, but each was amiable, suntanned, and as ordinary as the others in the tavern.

"Oyster, are you in or out?" Judd asked.

The slender fella lifted a finger and rotated his cards.

Judd rolled his eyes. "Not this again. Just play your blooming birds."

"Birds don't bloom," Oyster said softly. "Flowers do. And it's Zora's time to play her hand." He pushed ten silver coins into the growing pile in the center. "But like you, Judd, I'll call as well."

Zora sat up straight, smiled big, and spread her cards on the table. "Three cardinals and two crows."

Judd tossed his cards down. He had three sparrows, a robin, and a goldfinch. "Blooming rosebuds! I haven't won a hand in an hour."

Zora reached for the pile. "Don't be too down. I'm sure your fortune will change, but you better hope it changes before your purse is empty."

"Not so fast," Oyster said.

Zora's fingers stopped inches from the coins.

"This is getting interesting," Judd said as a barmaid handed him another tankard. He gulped it down and wiggled his bent ears. "Show her what you got, Oyster."

Oyster showed his cards one by one. "Woodpecker. Woodpecker. Woodpecker."

Zora's eyes grew like saucers.

"Goldfinch," Oyster said. He dangled the last card in his hand.

Judd leaned over the table. "If that's another goldfinch, I'm gonna pee myself." He eyed Oyster. "Enough of the suspense. Play it."

Oyster played his last card. "Robin."

A stunned silence fell over the table.

"Blooming rosebuds!" Judd said in disgust. "You blew it!"

Zora let out a relieved sigh, and she dragged the pile of

coins toward her. "I win again. It must be my lucky day. One more goldfinch and I'd have been a loser."

"Loser? You?" Moonlar asked in his deep voice. "You look like a winner to me, Zora. I salute you. Both of them always whip me, so it's good to see them lose for a change." He dropped his front chair legs on the floor and stood. "Pardon me. I need to relieve myself. No need to deal me in. I've lost enough wages today."

Zora stacked up her coins. Oyster shuffled the cards.

"You play well. I'll give you that," Judd said as he sipped on his ale.

"My father and I play all of the time." She looked at Crane, who was at the bar talking with the halfling barkeeper. "I've always had a knack for it. You don't think I took unfair advantage of you, do you?"

"Of course not," Judd said, "but I am embarrassed. However, I've enjoyed playing with a newcomer as lovely as you."

"Thank you."

"So, you and your father are passing through Red Bone, eh? Where are you from to begin with?"

This was the part in which Zora needed to be careful of the words she chose. She and Crane needed to be on the same page and share the same backstory. If they wanted to gain their new friends' trust, she needed to sound sincere and not be pushy. So far, they'd had a nice card game, but she hadn't learned anything that might be helpful. "We come from Raven Cliff, not far from here."

Judd nodded. "I like Raven Cliff. Been there many times myself, but I'm no fan of crossing the Iron Hills. Blooming goblins are nothing but trouble. I've been around Gapoli a time or two, but I'm from right here in Red Bone. Never too cold. I hate the cold."

She tucked her hair behind her ear and nodded. "We like the climate. I don't know if we'll put down roots here, but Father and I have tired of the northern atmosphere, if you know what I mean."

Oyster started dealing. Everyone received five cards.

Judd nodded. "Oh yeah, I know exactly what you mean. I hear the Black Guard are thicker than flies up there. Is that true?"

"They ruin everything. Well, at least we think so, but many people love the new direction, if you know what I mean," she said as she lifted her cards.

"Yeah, we get a lot of pass-throughs who say the same thing," Judd said as he drummed his fingers on his face-down cards. His tone darkened. "And that's the kind of remark that spies for the Black Guard make too. Tell me, who are you really, little sister?"

They're onto me. Got to sell it. She started to say something fast when she felt Oyster's dagger poke against her belly. *Goy! Where'd that come from?*

24

Zora kept her cool. "What's all of the hostility about, Judd? I don't serve Dark Mountain if that's what you're worried about. I'm only here to play cards."

"So you say, but how do we really know?" Judd nodded toward Crane. "The two of you stroll in here, and before long, you're buying drinks and talking like you own the place."

Moonlar the orc had returned from outside, and he stood at the bar dangerously close to Crane. His big hand was locked onto the pommel of his short sword.

"Uh, listen, I think I'm going to take my winnings and leave. I'm not going to be insulted. I thought you were nice men." She eyeballed Oyster. "Do you mind removing your pigsticker from my gut?"

Oyster's blade vanished into his scabbard in the wink of

an eye. He gave her an apologetic look. "She's not one of them, Judd."

"How can you be sure?"

"Because the Black Guard's minions aren't that good at cards or nearly as sincere and friendly."

"Yeah, I agree." Judd's knitted eyebrows eased, and he reached over and laid his hand on Zora's. "Accept my apology and stay, Zora. Give a hardhead another chance to win his money back."

"I don't know." She pulled her hand out from underneath his. "You startled me something awful."

The soft-spoken Oyster said, "Come now, Zora. You don't come across as one who frightens easily. After all, you seemed perfectly comfortable sitting with a rugged group like us."

"I've been around the horn, and no, I don't startle easily, but you did take me by surprise," she said. "You snuck that blade out in a wink, and that's not a sign of an ordinary man."

Oyster showed her a polite smile.

"He's quick and quiet, but that's about all." Judd dropped a tobacco pouch on the table, fished a large pinch of tobacco out, and stuck the wad in his jaw. "No wonder I'm edgy. I was so captivated by you and losing my chips that I forgot my chew." He made a sucking sound with his teeth. "That's better."

Moonlar waded through the tables, jostling customers

in their chairs with his big belly. "Pardon. Pardon." He returned to his chair. The wood beneath him popped and crackled, but the chair held. "I take it all is well."

"She's good," Judd said with a smile stained by tobacco. "As a matter of record, we were just apologizing."

Moonlar nodded. "Her paps makes fast friends too. He's talking Lola's ears off, and she's talking his off. They don't take a breath between sentences. I couldn't keep up with them."

"My father is very chatty," Zora agreed. "It runs in the family."

"Are you from a big family?" Oyster asked.

Goy! They're still vetting me! What if they work for the Black Guard?

"No, not really. My father and I are here, but my mother and sister are still in Raven Cliff." She stacked one small pile of coins on top of another. "We're seeking out a better place to live, but there's a bit of a dispute, as they still prefer Raven Cliff."

"That must be hard." Moonlar guzzled down his ale, threw his beefy arm up, and ordered another. "Dark Mountain has busted up many a family. We see new faces trying to settle in this territory all of the time, but the land is hard to work, unlike the green fields of the north."

"You can say that again. It didn't take us long to figure that out, and we aren't farmers, though Father wants to try it." She lifted her goblet when the barmaid refilled Moonlar's tankard. "I could use more wine, please."

Judd spoke up. "Well, let me go on the record and say that Red Bone is as good a place as any. I's born and raised here, same as these two, and we prefer it as to anywhere else. I hope that you and your father, uh..."

"Crane," she said.

"Yes, Crane, feel at home and welcome. Don't let the Black Guard spoil it for you. Ignore them. They won't last, I'm sure of it. I just hope to live long enough to see them gone." He raised a pint after Zora was refilled. "To the past. May it soon become our future."

"Hear! Hear!" Moonlar said in his deep voice. "Say, Zora, you said you crossed over the Iron Hills?"

"Er... yes," she said.

"We heard there was some trouble outside Raven Cliff," Moonlar continued.

"What sort of trouble?"

"I shoe horses for the Black Guard, and I heard them talking about an encounter with Doom Riders."

Her blood froze. "What sort of encounter?"

Moonlar stared deep into her eyes. "Supposedly, they were found dead. All of them. And they're searching for culprits."

Not good. Not good. Not good.

"That's only a rumor," Judd said, shaking his head. "Everyone knows that no one crosses a Doom Rider and lives. We've seen them before. Remember that one time they passed through?" He shivered. "I went the other way."

Oyster nodded. "I remember the day, years ago. I watched the streets clear as they passed."

Zora scratched her neck behind the Scarf of Shadows and told a white lie. "They sound frightening. This is the first I've heard about it, but if it's true, that's good, yes?"

"Not if you're the one who killed them," the big orc said. "You didn't hear anything about that?"

"Nope."

"Will you let it go?" Judd asked Moonlar. "You're going to draw trouble to us if you keep talking about the Doom Riders." He spit into an empty tankard. "The less we know, the better. If they are dead, we're all better for it. I'm certain. Now stop interrogating our friend, will you?"

Moonlar shrugged. "Sorry. But you know I like gossip. It's how I pass the time."

Zora's nose tingled. *Horseshoes! If they found the Doom Riders, they're probably coming after the gourn. I need to talk to Crane.* She took a big slug of wine. *Don't hurry off just yet.*

Zora picked up her cards. "Are we going to gossip or play cards, fellas?"

Moonlar knocked on the table. "I like both. Next hand, deal me in."

25

BACK IN THE COUNTRY BARN, Talon had engaged in a heated discussion.

"Let the gourn go. We don't need them," Razor argued. "Monsters like that are nothing by trouble anyway. Unlike a horse, they kill people."

Gorva stood with a gourn that had been stabled in the barn. She petted its nose. "They do what they are commanded to do. They are no more of a monster than a dragon is. It depends on the master."

Jakoby paced in a circle around a coal pit that burned low. "I agree with Gorva, but the gourn place us all in danger. As much as I enjoy the beasts, I think it's best that we let them go."

Crane rubbed his sagging jaw. "I don't think that's wise,

and we might be jumping to conclusions. Zora only heard a rumor. We don't need to jump out of our boots every time something someone says spooks us." He spread his arms. "We're safe here for the time being as long as we lie low."

The group started squabbling among themselves.

Zora captured every conversation. The company didn't need to die in order to save the gourn. It was too risky. They needed a safer place, and she agreed that the gourn put them in danger. It seemed like a novel idea at the time, but it had become risky. Yet her gut told her to keep the gourn.

"What are you thinking, Zora?" Crane asked.

"I think we need to be somewhere more remote. We're too close to the Black Guard and that Risker you mentioned," she said.

Crane nodded. "Yes, the Risker Lola described is bad news. We don't want to cross her. She's merciless, Lola said."

"You have a thing for the halfling ladies, don't you?"

"What's not to like? They're charming and adorable."

"Uh-huh."

Gorva marched into the center of the group and stood tall. "Everyone, listen to me!"

The barn quieted.

"Good, I have your attention. You cannot let these gourn go, and I'll tell you why." Gorva spoke with her husky orcen accent. "The gourn are similar to dragons.

What we did when we brought them into our service could be reversed against us. If the Black Guard capture the gourn, they could use them to hunt us down. I have no doubt they want the gourn so they can understand what happened to the Doom Riders. Like it or not, we're stuck with them."

Crane shrugged his eyebrows. "I never thought about that."

"Thank you, Gorva," Zora said.

All eyes fell on Zora. It gave her an uncomfortable feeling. She'd captured all of their attention, and she didn't understand why. She was the smallest in the group, but for some reason, they respected her voice.

"We appreciate the insight. We'll stay here a little longer. No sense in moving from our cover and getting caught if there's no need. Crane and I will head back to town tomorrow and try to verify if there's any truth to this rumor."

Razor waved his hands. "Wait a moment. Wait a moment." He sat in the back of the wagon and pointed his fingers at the ground. "I don't want to sit in this barn and rot along with the wood. I want to stretch my legs in Red Bone."

"No," Zora said.

Razor's dark eyes widened. "No?" He looked side to side and touched his chest. "Are you talking to me?"

"I am," she said. "What are you supposed to do, Razor? Limp into Red Bone carrying a dozen blades and telling stories about each and every one of them?"

"Hey! People like my stories!"

"Yes, people who are sleeping," Gorva said.

Razor gave Gorva a dangerous look. "Did you just make a joke?"

Gorva squared her shoulders. "I did."

Razor broke into gut-busting laughter and collapsed back into the wagon. The company broke out in smiles and chuckles.

"It's about time you loosened your sword belt, gorgeous." Razor sat up and wiped the tears from the corners of his eyes. "Oh, my ribs. They're still sore from trying to kill that Doom Rider's boots with them."

Gorva gave him a shoulder shove. "You're tough. You can take it."

Crane put his arm over Zora's shoulder. "You did well. Like I said, you're a natural."

She batted her eyes. "A natural what... beauty?"

He patted her rump. "That goes without saying, but know this, Tanlin was right about you. He'd be proud."

Zora wasn't sure exactly what Crane meant. Either that or she didn't want to admit it. But the words felt good. She scanned the weathered and weary faces in the room. It was a strong group of people, as strong as she'd ever known.

Am I their leader? I can't be. Can I?

"I think I'm going to take a walk. Get some fresh air," she said.

"Can I join you?" Crane asked.

"No, I need to be alone."

He stepped aside. "As you wish. It's a nice evening outside. Enjoy."

Zora quietly removed herself from the pack and squeezed through the barn door. It was a warm evening with a mild breeze, and the crickets chirped in soothing harmony. In the distance, she could see the farmer's cottage. A post lantern burned outside the front door. She brushed the hair from her eyes and glanced up at the stars.

So peaceful. Why can't it always be like this?

She distanced herself from the barn and headed for a grove of trees centered around a small watering pond. She sat down on the bank among the croaking frogs. They were loud.

Am I the leader of Talon now?

She remembered the likes of Adanadel and Dalsay, Browning and Tatiana, and of course, her fatherlike mentor, Tanlin.

I'm not like any of them. Am I? When Grey Cloak's back, I'm sure he'll take over.

She reached into her pocket and rubbed the dragon charm. It twinkled in her fingertips.

Does this have anything to do with it?

The frog song came to a stop. An eerie stillness fell over

the pond. The fine hairs on her earlobes tingled. She looked behind her. A group of dark figures in the shadows of the trees had her surrounded.

They closed in on her, and one of them said, "That's a pretty stone. Care if we have a closer look?"

26

ZORA CLOSED her fist over the charm. "Come any closer, and I'll use this stone to put an end to you."

"Whoa, little lady. Take it easy," someone said in a familiar voice. "We didn't mean to spook you."

"Judd?" she replied, referring to the man she'd played birds with. "Is that you?"

"Aye," Judd replied.

Two other men flanked him. The much bigger figure was the orc, Moonlar, and on his other side was Oyster, a man of slight build. All of them wore traveling cloaks, but Zora could see sword belts underneath.

"Again, apologies. It wasn't our intention to—"

She slowly rose, but she was hemmed in with her back to the pond. "To let me know you were going to rob me?"

"That's a dragon charm, isn't it?" the soft-spoken Oyster asked.

Zora's strengthened her voice. "That's not your concern. Back away. You're crowding me."

"I told you she was up to something," Moonlar said. His large, beefy hands clenched and unclenched. "She asks too many questions."

"Yes, we've established that Zora and her *father* were prying for information. It couldn't have been more obvious." Judd combed his fingers through his bushy hair. "Speaking of information, we have information that you might find helpful. That's why we came." Judd, though gruff looking, carried a convincing tone. "And a good thief can spot a good thief."

"Oh, so you are thieves?" she asked as she pulled one of her daggers from her hip. "Thieves with helpful information. And you came all the way out into the country to share it with me?"

"Sell it, actually," Oyster said. His arms were hidden in his robes, but his twinkling eyes were locked on the gemstone. "One dragon charm for information that will save your life."

"Sounds like a bargain. And all this time I thought you were a bunch of nice men. Instead, you only wanted to rob me and my father." The trio had her hemmed in good, but she had the Scarf of Shadows. *Keep them talking, and make a break for it.* "I'll tell you what, Judd. You share the information with me, and if it's worth my while, I might give you the charm."

"No, but I'll give you my word that if you give us the charm, we'll give you the information. How does that sound?"

"Awful. After all, I hardly even know you."

"We can always take it by force." Moonlar smacked his fist into his hand. "Three of us. One of you."

"Lay a hand on me, and you'll wish you'd never met me," she warned.

Judd let out a mirthful chuckle. "I like her. She has salt."

"And a dragon charm," said Oyster.

"Not to mention she's pretty too," Moonlar added.

"So we're in agreement, brothers?" Judd asked.

Oyster and Moonlar nodded.

Judd held up his hands and wiggled his fingers. "We had no intention to harm or rob you, Zora. I fear that we were only vetting you further. Please, keep your dragon charm. We don't want the trouble it brings. Now, allow me to properly introduce us." He took a bow. "We are the Rogues of Rodden. At your service."

"Seriously, you're the legendary Rogues of Rodden? I thought there were dozens of you."

"Used to be, but like many, we've fallen on hard times, and our ranks have been scattered and killed."

"Killed mostly," Oyster said.

She put her sword and dragon charm away. "Fine, I'll bite. So, what is this information that you have for me?"

"The Black Guard are seeking you out. The Risker, Hella, is too. Once they have your scent, they'll be coming," Judd said.

"What? Why?"

"It seems that your *father*, Crane, spoke a little too much to Lola," Oyster offered. "She's a Black Guard spy."

27

CRANE SAT in the back of the wagon, head down, with his legs hanging over the edge. His fingers were interlocked, and he was rolling his thumbs over one another. The barn was quiet. The Rogues of Rodden had entered, and introductions were made by Zora.

Crane lifted his head and eyed the others. "What is everyone looking at me for?"

"Because you blabbed," Razor was quick to say. He whisked two daggers out of their chest sheaths, spun them around, and sheathed them again in the wink of an eye. "And now I'm going to have to go without ale for who knows how many days? I was shot! I almost died, and I can't even get some warm mead."

"There are cows to milk in the barn," Gorva offered as she saddled her gourn. "Have some of that, you baby."

Razor shot her a look. "I'm not an orc. I don't drink fermented milk like you."

Gorva bowed up. "What did you say, human?"

"You heard me, gorgeous." Razor turned his back to her.

Gorva snorted.

"Crane, what did you say to Lola?" Zora asked.

"We chatted about things," he said with a guilty look. He caught the Rogues of Rodden looking at him. His brows knitted together over his soft eyes, and he slid off of the wagon. "Zora, are you going to take the word of strangers over mine? You only met them today. Not to mention they stole through the dark to attack you." He shrugged. "They admit they're part of a notorious band of thieves. Who are you going to believe, me or them?" He poked his finger at Judd.

"Crane, tell me what you said to Lola," she said in a firmer tone.

He gave her a disappointed look. "How do you know they aren't the spies?"

"I don't."

"Well, why am I being interrogated?" Crane asked. "You're treating me like I'm a spy and not them." He stormed out of the barn.

Zora raised her brow as she watched him go.

Jakoby moved in behind her. "I've never seen him flustered before."

"Or embarrassed," she said. Zora kept her other thoughts to herself. *He's getting older. He might be slipping.*

Judd scratched his bushy sideburns. "We aren't here to cause friction in your crew, Zora. The truth is, we knew that Lola was a spy. We keep our eye on that one. She can charm the toenails off an ogre once she gets you talking. Your father, Crane, well, I think she duped him. Nothing to be ashamed of."

Zora nodded.

Judd continued. "It wasn't long after you left that we saw Lola squirt out of the den. Oyster followed her." He jabbed a thumb at the soft-spoken rogue, who hadn't taken his eyes off the gourn. "Sure enough, she headed to her contacts with the Black Guard."

Oyster nodded. "I overheard them talking. Lola told them that Crane came across the dead Doom Riders on his trek from the north. The Black Guard want him for questioning. Lola assured them he'd be back in town on the morrow, that she didn't know where he went."

Judd eyed Zora. "It's good fortune. You have time to put some distance between you. When you don't show up tomorrow, they'll form a search party. No doubt Hella will be a part of that, and let me warn you, you don't want any part of Hella."

"But you do possess a dragon charm. It might save you," Oyster mentioned.

"Does she have a charm, or is she a true-blooded natural?" Zora asked.

Judd gave her a concerned look. "She's the real thing. Nasty. Of course, it seems like you've handled nasty before." He glanced at the gourn. "Anyone who can take down Doom Riders is a force to reckon with. Care to share the details of the battle?"

"No," Zora said.

Moonlar crept closer to Gorva. The oversized thief stood a hair shorter than the towering woman, but he had at least two hundred pounds on her, and a hundred pounds of that was fat belly. "Can I pet the gourn?"

Gorva had her hand firmly on the gourn's bridle. "Do so at your own risk."

Moonlar eased out a beefy palm and laid it on the gourn's nose. "He's warm as toast. His breath is steam." He ran his hand over the gourn's curled horn. "They're beautiful, like dragons. I always thought so. You are a fortunate woman to have such a beast."

The gourn snorted fire out of its nostrils and reared back off the ground a couple of feet.

Moonlar backed away with surprising grace for such a big man. "I've seen enough. Thank you."

"Listen, Zora. We like you. If we didn't, well, we'd have let you be," Judd said as he stuck some chew inside his cheek. "And we aren't supporters of Dark Mountain either. They represent everything freedom isn't."

"They cut into your pockets, eh," Razor said.

"They've done worse than that," Oyster said.

Judd continued. "As I was saying, we risked our own necks to warn you. Why? I don't know, but call it a gut feeling. We can't do anything to convince you, but you need to ride. I'd go south, as far as you can, as soon as you can." He spit juice on the ground. "Hella will find your scent if you keep your boots in the mud. Let's go, men."

Oyster made a polite bow, and Moonlar offered a friendly wave. They walked toward the open barn door and vanished into the night.

Judd was the last to leave. "We'll do what we can to throw them off. No doubt they will be questioning us." He winked at Zora. "To the blooming rosebuds."

She waved goodbye and gave them time to leave. *I better check on Crane.*

28

SAFE HAVEN

ANYA AND NATH led the way through the cave tunnels with Grey Cloak and Dyphestive trailing several steps behind. The tunnels were lit by small chips of minerals that shined with their own natural light. The stone floors were sandy, slick, and damp.

"How are you feeling, brother?" Grey Cloak asked. They'd been walking for hours.

Dyphestive shrugged his heavy shoulders. "The same as always, I reckon."

"And that's a good thing?"

"So long as I'm breathing."

"You looked awful. I've never seen you in such bad shape before. I didn't think you'd make it, but I'm glad you did."

Dyphestive patted his brother on the back. "I'm glad

you were there. I felt the poison working its way through my body. Something inside fought it, but it was losing, or I was losing. When it couldn't get any darker, I saw the light, a pure golden light. It destroyed the venom inside me." He offered his brother a sheepish smile. "I guess you've been there before too."

"You know it. Poison is nasty business. Thank goodness it hasn't taken us." Grey Cloak felt more alive than he'd felt in days. Having his blood brother back at his side gave him a feeling that perhaps the tide had begun to turn in their favor. Now they had Anya, Nath, Streak, and twelve dragons. It was a good start to build an army. "Well, brother, you look great. Your tan has returned, and you aren't pasty like the undead. I was worried."

"You worried?"

"Only a tad."

Dyphestive's heavy gaze fell on Anya. "She hasn't said much since I woke."

"Eh, well, things started to become frosty when you came out of your sleep."

"What do you mean?"

"I fear Anya has gone off the reservation the same as the other Sky Riders. She thinks she has enough dragons to take on Black Frost. Fourteen dragons against hundreds, not to mention Black Frost and his armies," Grey Cloak quietly said. He twirled the Rod of Weapons. "But I do have this, the figurine, and Drysis's eyeball. It's a good start."

"And the cloak?"

Grey Cloak brightened. "And the cloak! Yes."

He caught Anya glancing over her shoulder. He gave her a friendly wave. She frowned and turned away.

"Oh, and you have your sword."

"I do." Dyphestive moved the Iron Sword from one shoulder to the other. "I'm surprised you were able to save it. I would have forgiven you if you'd lost it... eventually."

"Good to know."

Nath hollered back, "We're getting close!"

Dyphestive hurried after Nath. "I wanted to thank you for healing me."

"You did that," Nath said in a scratchy voice that came and went. "No need to thank me again."

"Well, regardless, I'm grateful, Nath." Dyphestive offered his hand. "I owe you."

Nath shook his head. "You don't owe my anything, son. I do what I do because it's the right thing to do, not because I expect payment."

Dyphestive nodded.

"Anya was sharing her plan to defeat Black Frost's forces with me. Perhaps the two of you would like to hear it," Nath suggested.

This ought to be interesting, Grey Cloak thought. "Certainly, let's hear it."

The strong-willed woman strolled with her chin up and shoulders back. "It's a brilliant plan. We'll lure Black Frost's armies into the Shelf. Their forces will be divided, and with our advantage of knowing the terrain, we will destroy them."

"Do you really think there are enough of us to stops thousands if not tens of thousands of them? They'll swarm us like a hill of ants," Grey Cloak said. "There's not even a score of us, dragons and all."

"The Shelf will be our ally. Its landscape is treacherous, and its occupants are not fond of invaders," she said.

Grey Cloak felt spider legs crawling up his spine. "What occupants?"

"Hydras. Rock trolls. Great worms. Night bats. Creepers. Hoof lickers. Demon shades," Nath said. His list was very long and filled with creatures that Grey Cloak had never heard of before. "And giant badgers."

Grey Cloak adjusted the Cloak of Legends on his shoulders. "Well then, it sounds like you have it all figured out." He elbowed Dyphestive. "We have giant badgers, brother. The perfect army."

"Don't mock me, elf!" Anya's stare burned into him. "We've been fighting for our lives the last decade, and where have you been? All of a sudden you reappear, and you have a better plan."

"Well—"

"Well!" She stopped Grey Cloak in his tracks. "Well, what is your plan, General?"

"First, don't call me elf. Second, I'm a Sky Rider too.

Third, I prefer Grey Cloak, but if you're going to spit at me with every syllable"—he came nose to nose with her —"please, call me Grey!"

There was an uncomfortable moment of silence as they stared one another down.

"And here's my plan. It's to go back to the Wizard Watch and get rid of those underlings and rescue Tatiana. There!"

"Your plan is worse than mine. You won't make it within a league of the Wizard Watch, and most likely, Tatiana is dead. We know about the underlings. They are vicious."

"Agreed," Nath said. "Every bit as awful as Black Frost. Based on experience, I would say worse perhaps."

"Based on what experience?" Grey Cloak and Anya asked simultaneously.

"Oh," Nath said as his scratchy hermit voice cleared. "I haven't told you about that, have I?"

29

"I WAS A LOT YOUNGER THEN." Nath combed his fingers through his hair and led the way down the tunnel. His voice had fully cleared, and he didn't sound like a grumpy hermit anymore. "Young and naïve, like all of you. Ambitious but lacking the wisdom I needed at the time."

"What happened?" Dyphestive asked.

"And when did this happen?" Anya demanded.

Nath shrugged. "Oh, centuries ago, but I remember it the same as yesterday." His expression hardened. "Those underlings were almost the death of me. They are wicked, as wicked as I've ever seen. They summoned me to their world to dispatch one of their enemies called the Darkslayer."

Grey Cloak and Dyphestive exchanged knowing glances. The Darkslayer, or Venir rather, was the first hero they'd summoned with the Figurine of Heroes. Nath had mentioned knowing of him before, but he'd never told them about it.

"Go on," Grey Cloak said.

"I'm not going to go into the entire story, but I'll say this. The world those underlings come from will put hair on your chest." Nath eyed Anya. "It's a figure of speech. It won't actually happen."

"I know that," she said.

"Needless to say, we fought to our deaths only to join forces and conquer in the end. Fortunately, I found my way home." Nath grinned. "That adventure made me stronger. The Darkslayer taught me a thing or two. He made me tougher, something I would need down the road. I like to think that he learned from me too. As iron sharpens iron, men improve one another."

"So you fought. Who won?" Dyphestive asked.

Nath scratched his long fingernails over his heart. "If you want the answer to that, you'll have to ask him."

"This is bizarre. Portals. Other worlds. Thanks to the Wizard Watch, we have this madness," Anya sneered, stormed ahead, and separated herself from the men.

"She really is fiery, isn't she?" Nath asked with a head nod. "But well-meaning."

Grey Cloak started sorting through his thoughts out loud. "So, you've been to three worlds, all connected by the

Figurine of Heroes? Your world, my world, and the underlings' world."

"There are many worlds," Nath said in a dry voice. He cleared his throat. "Gads, my velvety voice comes and goes. I've no love for that. I'm not fond of sounding my age, let alone not looking it."

"So, your wife, Selene, has been summoned and your friend Bayzog, the elf?" Grey Cloak asked.

Nath nodded. "I miss them, and I thought Bayzog had passed, but given that the portal you are opening is, well, unpredictable, I suppose it's possible that these heroes or horrors can be summoned from any point in time." He rubbed his chin and raised a finger. "But I wonder, are they shades of what they were, or is it actually them? Selene appeared to have been from my time. I'm certain of it, but I'm not certain about Bayzog. I didn't see him." He gently elbowed Dyphestive in the ribs. "They were something back then. I long to be reunited with both of them, especially my wife."

"We'll get you back," Dyphestive said.

"I hope, because I'm not getting any younger, and Black Frost's power drains my world and me every day. I grow weaker, and that's not easy for me to admit, but it's obvious to look at me. Typically, I look as spry as either of you and far more handsome."

"Yes, I believe you've mentioned that before." Grey

Cloak turned his attention to Anya. She'd moved far ahead of them. "We're running out of time, aren't we?"

"What do you mean?" Nath asked.

"Every day, you grow weaker, and Black Frost grows stronger. It didn't help that we lost the last ten years. That only made matters worse." He watched Anya's hair bounce side to side across her back. "No wonder she's so mad. No wonder she wants to strike now."

"A wise man from another world once said, 'He who hesitates is lost,'" Nath said.

Grey Cloak gave him an aggravated look. "How many worlds have you been to?"

Nath started counting on his fingers and moved to his second hand.

"Never mind," Grey Cloak said. "I'm going to catch up with Anya."

He jogged ahead and heard Dyphestive say, "I'd like to hear more about these worlds."

Nath replied, "Certainly."

Grey Cloak caught up to Anya and slowed to a walk. "How about a truce?"

"I'm not at war with you. I'm at war with Dark Mountain," she replied.

"You know what I mean." *Goy, she's such a hothead.* "Anya, I understand where you're coming from. It might have taken me a long time to get on board with the idea of the need to end this fast, but I am now. I realize we're running out of time."

"So glad that you're finally *on board*."

"Did I just hear your eyes rolling up into your skull when you said that?" he asked as tried to look into her eyes.

She looked away. "Stop that."

"Stop looking into those pretty blue eyes?"

"Do you want me to cut your tongue out?"

"I was only trying to draw a smile. You can still do that, can't you?"

"I'll smile when Black Frost is dead."

"Speaking of frosty." Grey Cloak shivered. "Before you decide to draw Black Frost's attention to us all, let's sit down and weigh all of our ideas together. What do you say?"

"I can't think of another way."

"Well, maybe I can. Maybe we can."

"I'll think about it."

The tunnel opened into a massive lair of rock formations covered in all sorts of colorful vegetation as far as the eye could see. A lake contained swimming ducks and jumping fish. Waterfalls spilled from an unknown source above. Huge stones that shined like daystars bathed the rich subterranean land in warm light.

"Whoa," Grey Cloak said. "It's beautiful."

A distant roar of a dragon caught his attention. He looked upward. A gorgeous middling dragon glided across the sky-like ceiling hundreds of feet above. She was an elegant middling with bright pink in her scales and around her eyes. Streak chased after her. They did twists and turns in a playful manner through the air.

Streak caught Grey Cloak's eye, dove, and soared right by his face. "That's my sister, Feather. Isn't she great?"

With her arms crossed, Anya led the way down into the picturesque valley. "Welcome to Safe Haven. It seems we have a lot of introductions to make."

30

RED BONE

THE ROGUES of Rodden returned to Lola's Tavern the next day. They sat at a small table near the middle of the half-empty rotting establishment. Judd and Moonlar each had a plate of steaming boar meat with hot rolls and a bowl of gravy to dip it in. Two pitchers of ale sat in the middle of the table, and Moonlar refilled their pints.

Meanwhile, Oyster, who didn't eat, shuffled a deck of bird cards with his nimble fingers. He set three cards faceup on the table, an eagle card in the middle and two crow cards on the sides. He flipped them facedown and rotated them quickly with one hand. "Follow the eagle, Moonlar. Two silvers says you can't find it."

Moonlar groaned. He dipped his roll into the gravy, stuffed it in his mouth, and chewed. He intently watched the cards. "I hate this game. I never win."

"Go ahead, pick. It's for my sake. I need my practice, and it's only two chips. You can spare that," Oyster said quietly.

"No." Moonlar tucked a cloth napkin into his jerkin. "You aren't making a fool out of me today."

Judd sat with his back to the bar, where Lola was busy at work serving and talking up her customers. He eyed Oyster. "Is that dirty little acorn watching us?"

Oyster made a subtle nod. He rubbed under his nose. "Indeed."

"Moonlar, you need to play along with Oyster. We don't want that dirty little lip-reader to get suspicious of us," Judd said.

"Are you going to pay back the coin I lose?" the beefy orc responded.

"You know Oyster will give it back."

Moonlar let out a gusty laugh. "That will be the season. Fine, I'll play along." He studied the cards and tapped the one in the middle. "That one!"

"Put up the chips," said Oyster.

"Ugh." Moonlar reached into the side pocket of his vest and produced a pair of chips. He flicked them on the table. "There, take them. I'll lose anyway."

"If you insist." Oyster swept the coins off the table and flipped the middle card over. It was an eagle. "Tsk. Tsk. You should have stuck with your gut."

"Gah!" Moonlar slapped his face. "One day I'll figure you out."

"How's your meal, fellas?" Lola asked. The pretty little halfling twirled her chestnut hair around her finger while standing on a meal cart pushed by a bare-armed half-orc brute in a greasy apron. The elevation gave her a slight advantage in height over two of the three sitting men.

"Good as always, Lola," Judd answered. "You serve the best hog in town. That's why we practically live here, right?"

Moonlar nodded. "Right."

"That's good," Lola replied in her buttery voice. She opened up a small beige fan decorated with flowers and added, "A shame it's always so hot in here. Some days I can barely stand it. So." She rocked on her heels. "I was curious. The half elf, Zora, you played birds with the other day, have you seen her about?"

Judd met Lola's eyes. He knew exactly what she was doing, watching his eyes, trying to catch him in a lie. He had to play it carefully. That was why he'd told the other two he would do the talking. "Not since yesterday," he said. "Any particular reason you ask?"

"Well, I was fond of her father, Crane. He's a very interesting man, and he said he'd return today. He seemed like a man of his word, and I thought he'd be here about now." She added a frown and a head tilt.

"Sounds like he made an impression on you, Lola. I didn't think you took such a shine to strangers," Judd said.

She shrugged her tiny shoulders. "Well, every so often someone special comes around. One never knows." She closed her fan. "I imagine he's still looking around Red Bone for a place to live."

"Did he mention that he had a wife?" Judd inquired. "'Cause Zora said they were looking for her family." The more truth he fed her, the more likely she would trust his word. His mentor had once taught him a valuable lesson. *You can't lie if it's true.* He studied the disappointed expression on her little face. "Sorry, I guess he didn't mention that. I suppose I shouldn't have either. Heh, you know how men are." He took a long drink from his pint.

Lola offered a warm smile. "Perhaps that's why he didn't come back. A shame. Wife or no, I liked him." She winked at Judd. "I'm sure we could have worked something out. I only wish I knew where he was headed. I'd like to say goodbye in my own special way. Did Zora mention any other places they might be looking?"

Oyster started shuffling the cards from hand to hand, but he remained slouched over the table. Moonlar sucked down more brew.

"She said they had more family in Havenstock," he lied, "and they might cross back over the Iron Hills." He refilled his pint. "That's all I recall." He shrugged. "Sorry for your fortune, Lola. But if I see them—"

"I know, you'll let me know." Her smile straightened. She nodded at the orc behind her cart. "Let's move. I have some errands to run." She flipped her hair. "A tavern owner's life is so very busy." A few moments later, she was gone.

Moonlar let out a gasp.

"What were you doing, holding your breath?" Judd asked the orc.

"I wanted to make sure I didn't say anything. I kept wanting to say south," Moonlar said.

"I don't know how you ever became a rogue. You're a horrible liar and sneak," Judd said.

"He's the muscle," Oyster offered.

Judd scratched his bushy sideburns. "Do you think she bought it?"

"I don't know," Oyster said as he set the deck down on the table. "She left rather quick."

"Yeah, I noticed that, too, and for some reason, my elbows are itching." He cut the deck. "Let's drink, and you deal."

31

JUDD NOTICED Lola returning a couple of hours later empty-handed. She appeared from the kitchen behind the bar in the back of her tavern. Her chubby cheeks were flushed, and her eyes were jittery. The men were playing cards, and a small pile of chips sat as the centerpiece of their table.

Judd rearranged his hand of cards and said underneath his breath, "Look who's back."

Oyster nodded. "I see, and I raise you both." He dropped five silver chips on the table.

"Here we go again," Moonlar said. "Well, I have a hand I know you can't beat. I'll see your five chips and raise you five more. Moonlar is going to sleep well tonight, at least after a few more pints." He winked at Oyster. "At your expense, of course."

Judd dropped his chips on the table and tossed down

his cards. "A pair of sparrows." Out of the corner of his eye, he could see Lola walking across the top of the bar while wringing her hands. She was bossing her staff around, and they'd begun cleaning, wiping down the bar and hurrying to clear the empty tables. He spit in a brass spittoon on the floor. "I believe someone is expecting company."

"Maybe we should vacate," Oyster suggested.

"No one is going anywhere, not until I play this hand. I've been waiting all day to win a big one," Moonlar said. "Show me your birds."

"As you wish." Oyster laid down three of his five cards faceup. "Three robins."

Moonlar leaned over the table and grinned. "Three hawks!" He dropped his cards. "Heh, that beats your little robins." He reached for the pile of coins.

"No so fast," Oyster warned him. He flipped another card over. It was a fourth robin. "A full nest of robins." He dropped his fifth card. "And one eagle." He stretched his fingers over the coins. "It looks like I'll be sleeping well tonight."

The muscles in Moonlar's jaw flexed. He ground his teeth. "Touch those coins, and I'll break your hand off."

"Don't start this now," Judd warned.

"I'm not starting anything. I'm finishing it." His expression eased, and he flipped a fourth hawk on the table. "Bwah-huh-huh-huh-huh!" His belly jiggled. "I got you! I got you, fish head!" He swept the pile of coins toward his chest. "I got you good!"

Two Black Guard soldiers entered through the front door of the tavern. They posted themselves on each side of the entrance. Every man and woman turned and looked. Loud conversations turned to curious murmuring.

Judd kept his voice low and said, "It looks like we're going to have company. Stick to the story, and let me do the talking. I can handle them." He'd taken his eyes off the door for a moment. When he returned his gaze to the Black Guard, the hairs on his wooly arms stood on end. "Blooming rosebuds," he uttered.

An imposing woman with striking features stepped through the entrance. Dead silence fell over the room. It was Hella, the Risker. Her jet-black hair was frizzy and stood on her head like a crown. Stylish black streaks were painted underneath her penetrating eyes. She wore a full black suit of dragon armor, customary of her ilk. Wolf fur lined the cape draped over her shoulders. One hip was dressed with a sword, and the other showed a whip. Blades were strapped to her ankles.

"Yes, yes, you do the talking," Moonlar suggested in a shaky voice.

Judd's chest tightened the moment she set eyes on him.

The rickety boards groaned underneath Hella's feet as she ventured deeper into the tavern. Her eyes had not left Judd or his table. She stopped only a foot away, pulled back an empty chair, and set her foot on it. She leaned forward, broke eye contact with Judd, started to slip off her gauntlets, and in a strong voice that carried across the room, she calmly said, "I'd like to talk to these three men alone."

Every patron in the tavern scrambled for the front door like rats on a sinking ship. They knocked chairs over on their way out, and in a few moments, every table and barstool was abandoned save for one.

Judd heard Moonlar swallow.

Hella scooped up their playing cards in her strong fingers, and without looking at any one of them, she began to shuffle the deck. "I used to love to play cards when I was a child. Not so much anymore." She bent the thick deck in half with her fingers, flexing the cards. "But I had to learn to focus on more important matters, life-and-death matters."

32

Hella remained standing and started dealing the cards facedown, one each to the three men. The remaining cards in her hand began to disintegrate in her palm. "Each of you has a card. When you flip them over, the person with the highest-ranking card will be interrogated first."

"Interrogated?" Judd asked.

Hella's smile was as white as ivory behind her wine-colored lips. "Of course, you can all avoid interrogation so long as you share with me your entire conversation with the half elf, Zora. I want to know where she and her father, Crane, went."

"Uh... no disrespect, but we don't know," Judd offered. He could feel sweat dripping down the side of his cheek.

Beside him, Moonlar was sweating raindrops, more so than he normally did.

"Certainly you men are aware that I'm not the sort of person to be trifled with. You've seen or heard what I do to people, haven't you?" she asked.

Judd and Moonlar nodded.

She set her gaze on Moonlar. "Tell me, fat belly, what have you heard?"

"You feed them alive to your dragon," the sweaty orc replied.

"Or?" she asked.

"The dragon burns them alive," Moonlar added with a stammer. "Some loose lips are allowed to live as an example of your... mercy?"

"Well spoken, orc. Now, would any of you like to offer some helpful information before the actual interrogations begin? And don't take a lot of time to think about it. I'm a busy woman. I don't like delays, but I'll give you some time." She looked at her fingernails, which were polished a glossy black. "Hurry now."

Gooseberries! Judd knew enough about the Riskers and their ilk to know that they weren't to be trifled with. Some of them were only men, but the ones like Hella were naturals. They were a different breed entirely. Faster, stronger, smarter than the others, and users of magic. *This is what I get for trying to help a pretty woman.*

"Time's up. Nothing?" she asked.

Judd and Moonlar shrugged. Oyster sat as still as a deer.

"I see. Well, flip your cards over. It's time to start."

All three men did as she requested. Oyster had a sparrow. Judd showed a hummingbird, and Moonlar, the high card, a black crow. The orc leaned back in his chair with his eyes as wide as saucers.

Hella stepped off her chair and uncoiled her whip. "You look nervous, fat belly? Why is that?"

Eyeing the whip, Moonlar said, "I-I've never been interrogated before."

She cracked the whip.

Wupash!

"Don't worry. I'm certain you'll hate it. Black Guard, seize him!"

The Black Guard hooked Moonlar behind the arms and tried to lift him out of his seat. Moonlar balled up. One of the soldiers smote him in the back of the skull with his dagger pommel. The orc sagged in his chair and collapsed onto the floor.

"You knocked him out, fool!" Hella said. She gave the soldiers a look of disgust. "My patience is lost." She pulled the whip back and let it fly.

Judd dove out of his chair. The whip cracked over his back.

Wupash!

He climbed to his feet just in time for a second strike of the whip to coil around his neck. Hella yanked him off his feet and sent him crashing through a set of chairs and tables, knocking food and brew all over the floor.

She stepped on his chest and pulled the whip tight. "Listen, fool! I've toyed with you long enough. Tell me where the woman has gone! I know you know something! I can see it in your eyes!"

He made a feeble gesture with his hands and shook his beet-red face.

"You left town last night. You came back later!" she said. "Where did you go?"

How'd she know that? Judd noticed Lola peeking from behind the end of the bar. *That dirty halfling is going to get us all killed.* He wedged his finger in between the whip and his neck and pulled. He stuck with what he knew and managed to say in a strained voice, "I don't know where she is." It was a true statement. He didn't know exactly where Zora was.

Hella's hot glare could have burned a hole in him. She kicked him in the ribs several times. "Tell me! Tell me! Tell me!"

Judd had been in his fair share of scrapes over the years, but this woman was going to beat the life out of him. Using the whip, she towed him across the floor. He was choking.

She stopped and pulled the whip harder. "Fine, I'll kill you and ask the next."

A sharp metal dagger streaked through the air and cut the whip.

Snip.

Hella stumbled backward and fell through a table.

Judd tore the whip away from his neck and started coughing.

Oyster helped him to his feet and said quietly, "These people must be really important."

He nodded. "I'm gumming up."

"Agreed."

Hella rose with fury in her face. She had food all over her armor. "You've made your decision. There won't be any mercy now." She drew her blade. The sword blade glowed like fire. "I'm going feed you both to my dragon." She came at them.

Moonlar's arm swept across the ground and took her feet out from under her. Before she could get up, he pounced on her back.

"We should run," Oyster suggested.

"True, but you know we can't." Judd drew his broadsword.

Oyster's hands filled with short lengths of steel.

"At least we can buy our new friends some time. It's been good knowing you, brother."

"Agreed," Oyster replied as he touched the flat of his daggers to his chin. "Remember the Rogues of Rodden!"

Judd charged, shouting, "Remember the Rogues of Rodden!"

Hella exited Lola's tavern minutes later with blood on her face and armor. Her nostrils flared. The scowling woman shook the gore from her blade and slammed it into its sheath. Facing the troops of the well-armed Black Guard, she said, "Knock down every door in this town, and find out where those men were last night." She glanced over her shoulder. "And burn this rathole down."

TALON TRAVELED south at a brisk pace, baking in the hot midday sun. They were surrounded by sloping hills and rocky terrain, where the sparse vegetation worsened league by league. Overhead, carrion vultures circled beneath the patches of clouds.

Zora rode in the wagon, sitting beside Crane. The others were in the front, on gourn or horseback, with Jakoby and Gorva leading the way. Leena and Razor rode just behind the lead.

Crane dabbed his face with a navy-blue handkerchief. Sweat dripped off his chin, and even his plum robes had sweat stains in the armpits. He'd said little since they'd made a hasty exit from the barn, which wasn't like Crane at all.

"Do you want to talk?" Zora asked.

Slouched over, Crane shrugged.

"It really makes me uncomfortable when I don't hear your cheerful voice. Please, say something," she pleaded.

The wagon rocked over a rut in the road and pitched to one side.

Zora slid into Crane, caught herself, and squeezed his arm. "Crane, come on. We need you."

He had the sad look of a defeated man. "I'm slipping."

"What? You? What are you talking about?" she asked.

"You don't have to protect me, Zora. You know what I did." He looked up at the others in the lead. "They know what I did. I slipped. I can't slip. I'm Crane."

She patted his knee. "All of us slip from time to time."

"Not me." He tightened his lips and shook his head. "That little halfling witch duped me. I never thought for a moment she was a spy. I think I have a weakness for halflings." He glanced at Gorva. "And orcs." He looked at Zora. "And half elves."

"You have a weakness for women."

"See? I'm slipping!"

"Honestly, Crane, how many times have you slipped before? How many secrets have you passed on to a woman of surpassing beauty?"

"Er, well, none, aside from that little dickens, Lola." His sagging cheeks turned up into a smile. "Boy, she was cute. And that personality and those tight little—"

"Crane!"

"Sorry. See? I'm slipping." He rubbed his mouth. "My, I'm thirsty all of a sudden." He reached back into the wagon and grabbed a wine skin. "With any luck, it will rot my tongue off, and I won't be able to betray the company anymore."

Zora smiled. At least she had him talking again. That was a relief. Now all she needed to do was get his confidence back. "It's in the past. We can only move forward now. You need to forget about it."

"How can I? Lola haunts my dreams. The dirty little halfling has ruined me."

"Have you ever gotten over a woman before?"

He nodded.

"Then you'll get over this one too."

Crane's face brightened. "You know, I think I will. Thanks, Zora. So, you forgive me?"

"There's nothing to forgive."

"What about them?" he asked.

"I have a feeling this incident is the furthest from their mind. We had to move on anyway."

"Yes, but if a Risker comes with a small army, well, it might not turn out well for us," he said. "I don't want death by dragon. I want to die in peace with a gorgeous halfling or two tucked in my arms."

"What about Gorva?" she playfully asked.

"She can tuck me in her arms."

Zora let out a delighted giggle. "You're shameless."

"I know. I feel bad. Sometimes." He scanned the horizon. "There's a river to the west of us. It leads to Dwarf Skull. I'm not so certain that's the safest route, but it looks like that's the direction Jakoby is heading."

"You know that land better than any. What do you think?"

"A stop at the river won't hurt. It will be good to water the horses. We can weigh our options there."

"That's the Crane I know."

He nodded.

A few hours later, the company came to a stop along a rocky riverbank. Everyone dismounted, stretched their legs, and watered their mounts.

The river was wide, and the waters moved fast.

Jakoby skipped a flat stone over the water. "We need to find a safe place to cross. We'll follow the river farther south. I'd imagine there's a crossing every league or so." He eyed Crane. "Isn't there?"

"Yes, yes," Crane agreed. "But we don't want to take our troubles to Dwarf Skull."

Jakoby eyed him. "Where are we supposed to go, then? We have allies in Dwarf Skull."

"Yes, but that doesn't mean there aren't Riskers. We can't ride into Dwarf Skull with gourn. It will draw too much attention. We need to hide." He massaged his jaw. "We need to vanish."

"How do you suppose we do that?" Gorva asked.

"I know a place," Crane suggested. "Crow Valley."

"Crow Valley, huh?" Razor asked. "I hear that's nothing but a pile of rocks."

"And caves," Crane added. "Lots of caves."

Hella strolled through the barn that Talon had occupied. Her hand grazed a support beam. She called out, "Steelhammer!"

A grand dragon stuck his massive head through the barn door opening. He had great horns that curled into a point. His scales were dark, peppered with bright-silver markings, with many hard ridges on his nose and around his burning silver eyes. His resonant voice shook the barn when he spoke. "Yes, dear Hella?"

"Do you have the scent?"

Steelhammer inhaled deeply through his nostrils. "You smell wonderful."

"Don't toy with me. You know I'm not in the mood."

"Of course not, dearest one. I have their scent. Each and every one. Get on," Steelhammer said. "We'll catch them in no time, no time at all."

34

SAFE HAVEN

GREY CLOAK and Anya found Cinder resting in the serenity of the valley. There were three middling dragons with him, all female, with lighter scales on their chests. They were identical aside from the splashy colors on their scales. One had red, the second white, and the third blue scales that matched their pretty eyes.

"These are my daughters," Cinder said proudly. "We call them the Triplets. Adorable, aren't they?"

For some reason, Grey Cloak tingled all over. He nodded. "Gorgeous, like their mother."

The Triplets nestled closer to their father, who'd sprawled out on the soft grass of the unique flowery terrain.

"They can act shy, but don't let them fool you. That's only what they want you to think." Cinder winked at him.

Dyphestive and Nath climbed down a step-like formation and joined them. Dyphestive had a broad smile on his face.

"What have you two been talking about?" Grey Cloak asked.

"A lot," Dyphestive said with an excited grin. He eyed the three dragons. "Who are these pretty ladies?"

The dragon girls purred and rattled their tails.

"These are the Triplets," Anya responded. "Cinder, if you will, please summon the rest of your brood. I'd hate for them to come upon our guests and accidentally eat them."

"Certainly." Cinder stretched his great neck upward and let out a calm but loud roar. "The dragon call should have them all here shortly."

Nath crossed his arms. "We'll see about that."

Feather and Streak were the first to touch down from the air.

"What's going on, Father?" Feather asked politely.

"We are making introductions, daughter," Cinder said. "This is Grey Cloak and Dyphestive. You know, the ones we've talked about."

Feather nodded. "Nice to meet you both. Welcome."

"Uh, thank you," Dyphestive said with a bow. "I like your pink scales. They are gorgeous."

"Thank you, friend."

The ground trembled. From a nearby cave, two grand

dragons approached on foot. "That's Fenora with the eyes like jade, and Bellarose with lavender eyes."

"They're big for girl dragons," Dyphestive said with round eyes.

"You can say that again," Feather said.

The Triplets sniggered in their own dragon way.

"Shame, Feather. You should know better," Anya said, but she cracked a smile.

Fenora arrived with Bellarose trudging along far behind her. "What's going on, Father?" Fenora asked.

"I wanted you to meet our extended family, Grey Cloak, Dyphestive, and your long-lost brother, Streak."

"Another brother?" Fenora asked in a sassy voice. "Oh, that's great. As if six wasn't enough. No offense, Streak, but your brothers are a bunch of turds."

Aghast, Feather said, "Fenora, language!"

"You aren't the boss, little pinky," Fenora responded.

When Bellarose wandered up, her yawning mouth was as big as a cave. She let out a long sigh, blinked her sleepy lavender eyes, and said, "What's going on, Father? I was sleeping."

"Bellarose, we have some guests," Cinder said.

Bellarose looked the group over. "That's great. Can I go back to sleep now?"

"You look like you're asleep already," another dragon said.

Grey Cloak glanced up at a formation of rocks and

noticed a sleek middling dragon gathered on the rocks who was doing the speaking. He had pitch-black eyes flecked with silver. He scurried down the rocks like a lizard.

"Oh, look who's here, Slick Spot," Fenora said with an eye roll. "The black sheep of the family."

"At your service, and it's only *Slick*." The fast-talking dragon stood on his hind legs and took a bow. "So, a gathering of epic-less proportions." He put his wing over Dyphestive's shoulder. "Don't listen to my sisters. They are extremely jealous of their brothers, who more or less dominate them."

"Do not!" Fenora yelled. "I'm going to turn you into a greasy stain, Slick. Just you wait!"

"Here we go again," Feather said to Grey Cloak. "I try to keep the peace, but well, they're really immature most of the time."

"Really, children. Is this the sort of impression that we want to impose on our new friends?"

Bellarose yawned. "I don't really care. I only want to go back to sleep. Can I be dismissed, Father? I was in the middle of this dream about a giant possum-man-dragon-thing..."

Slick jumped in front of Cinder and clasped his claws together. "Father, please let her go. You know those dream stories drive all of us crazy. Remember the last time, she cornered us for a week. A week, Father! I can't take another week!"

Streak's eyes were bright with enthusiasm. He wagged both of his tails.

Fenora locked her gaze on Streak. "Say, why does he have two tails?" She crept toward the much smaller dragon and looked him over. "That's weird. I don't remember you being born with two tails. I remember one. Only one of us has two tails."

"Let it go, Fenora. You're being rude," Feather said.

"Spare me. He's family. He better get used to it." Fenora nudged Streak with her tail. "So, where'd you get that tail? Dragons don't have two tails. And you were a runt. How'd you get so big? Huh, little brother? Huh? Huh? Huh?"

Streak got nose to nose with her. "Maybe it's none of your business. Did you think about that?"

Fenora narrowed her eyes. "I could eat you in one bite, runt."

The spines on Streak's stripes rose. "I'd like to see you try."

35

"THAT'S ENOUGH, Fenora and Streak. There will be time enough to wrestle later," Cinder said.

Fenora bumped noses with Streak. "Lucky for you."

"Say, what's going on, Dad?" Another middling dragon entered the picture. His belly dragged over the ground as he approached. Unlike the other dragons, his eyes were dull brown, matching the flare in his scales. He sniffed Grey Cloak. "Who are these fellas?"

"Chubby, this is Grey Cloak, his blood brother, Dyphestive, and your brother, Streak," Cinder replied.

"Whoa, another brother? That makes seven of us to six girls. Woohoo!" Chubby was elated.

"Don't get so excited, big belly," Fenora said. "There could be twenty of you, and you still wouldn't be a match for us."

Chubby stuck his tongue out and blew a raspberry. "Welcome, brothers! It's good to meet you."

"Very good to meet you," someone hissed in a velvety voice.

Grey Cloak and Dyphestive twisted around.

Another dragon wandered into the group. He was a middling with cobalt-blue eyes and flares on his scales. He sat on his hind legs and clicked his long black talons together like he was sharpening knives. He smiled, revealing rows of razor-sharp teeth. "I'm Slicer. The best of the bunch." He crept up on the young man and elf and got in their faces. He sniffed them and flashed his talons. "I can carve you up, roast you, and serve you in a matter of moments."

"Slicer, they're on our side," Cinder warned with an eye roll. "You'll have to forgive my children. They've never been out of the Shelf and aren't savvy to the nature of the rest of the world."

"I only want to kill something," Slicer said with his brows knitted together. "We are dragons. We can't keep feeding on underworld monsters and giant badgers. We need flesh, a challenge. These two bags of fleshy bones will do."

"I'm sure you'll get your chance to fight soon enough," Grey Cloak said. "After all, there are hundreds of dra—"

Anya clamped her hand over his mouth and whispered, "Hush. They don't know the entire story."

"Oh," he said, "well, what do they know?"

"We'll handle that. It's a very delicate situation," Nath added. "They've been trained, but for what, they don't know. The truth is, we don't know either."

The towering form of Fenora looked down on them. "Feather, I think we might want to let them know that, you know, we know."

Feather nodded. "Yes, we've known. We've always known. We know about the Day of Betrayal, Black Frost, the death of our mother, Firestok, and the Horror at Hidemark. We've known all of it for a long time." She gave Cinder a sheepish look. "Sorry, Father."

Cinder tilted his head to one side. "How do you know?"

"Well, as you can see, there isn't much to do around here, so we eavesdrop, a lot." Feather grinned. "Sorry."

Cinder gave her a disappointed look.

"Well, honestly, you could have been more careful, Father," Fenora said.

Cinder gasped. "What? More careful? We only spoke in privacy."

"Yeah, well, when you thought we were off playing or hunting, one of us would, you know, sneak around to listen to what you were saying," Slicer added. "Sometimes it was me."

"And sometimes it was me," Slick said with a coy smile. "Well, most of the time."

"I was in on it," Feather admitted.

Cinder looked down at the Triplets. They looked away. "Not my little babies."

Anya blew a wavy strand of hair out of her eyes. "Well, so much for that."

Nath let out a raspy laugh. "Children. So full of surprises. They know more than we are willing to give them credit for."

"How long have you known?" Cinder asked.

"Years," Feather said.

"Yeah, it's time to take the gauntlets, Father, and start training us for real battle," Fenora said with a firm head shake. "We're ready to avenge our family."

Slicer clicked his onyx-colored talons together. "Yeah, more than ready."

The ground shook.

Thoom.

The cave tremored.

Thoom.

Grey Cloak scanned the area. "What's that?"

"Great. Here comes Big, Slow, and Stupid," Fenora said.

Grey Cloak tapped Fenora. "Do you mind?"

"Sure. Climb aboard."

Grey Cloak climbed up her back and stood between the horns on her head. Dyphestive did the same on Cinder.

Three grand dragons approached from different directions. One was as bulky and burly as the next, each as big as Cinder if not bigger. The one in the middle pounded his paws into the ground as he walked, shaking everything in his path.

Streak hovered in the air, wings beating. "Whoa. Who are they?"

Feather rose up beside him. "That's Smash in the middle. He likes to make noise."

"A real drama dragon," Fenora said.

"See the one with that giant tooth sticking up out of his mouth? That's Snags," Feather added. "Looks silly, doesn't he?"

"Looks fierce," Dyphestive said.

"Huh," Fenora disagreed.

"I used to call him Fang, but someone convinced me to rename him." Cinder looked down at Nath.

Nath gave him a thumbs-up and said with a smile, "Fang's taken!"

"So, who's the last one?" asked Grey Cloak.

The last one had a huge shovel-shaped head with short spiky horns on the top of his skull. His granite scales made him look like he was chiseled from stone.

"That's Rock. He's the oldest by a day before me. A real charmer," Fenora scoffed.

Grey Cloak nodded as he looked at his brother. It had been a long time since they'd been around so many dragons together. The last time, they were young, taking care of a multitude of dragons in the Kennels. He'd seen all sorts of dragons back then. They were mostly the same with a few variations, but the children of Cinder and Firestok were different. He wasn't sure what it was, but in his gut, he knew they were unique. They gave him hope.

Smash, Snags, and Rock came closer. They stood eye to eye with their father and searched the faces of the newcomers.

Rock said in a resonant and rugged voice, "Are these the guys?"

"These are the ones," Cinder said.

"It's time to fight, isn't it, Dad?"

Cinder nodded. "I believe the time has come."

Rock nodded. "Good."

36

SULTER SLAY

THE DAYS WERE hot and the faces long, and there had been a lot of grumbling with the company opting to travel east to Crow Valley instead of traveling to Dwarf Skull. They moved at a trot.

Zora chose to follow Crane's instruction. It wasn't an easy choice either. She would have loved to see Rhonna again, but she knew she couldn't let her heart get in the way of her head. That was a lesson Tanlin had taught her in life. It had taken a long time for it to sink it, but as she'd matured, it had finally stuck and seasoned her.

For miles ahead, there was nothing but bright sun and barren land. Watery mirages that tempted the tongue appeared on the horizon only to vanish and reappear on the next horizon. The trek through the endless leagues of rugged wasteland wore down Talon's spirits. No one was talking. The only smiles came from the cracks in the sand.

Zora reached back into the wagon and picked up a waterskin. She shook it. "Not much left in this one."

"It's a good thing that we filled up at the river because we won't be seeing another one for quite some time," Crane admitted.

Zora had been to Crow Valley before, long ago when she'd first ventured with Grey Cloak, but she didn't remember the journey being so far. Perhaps that was because they hadn't been being chased and she hadn't been in charge. "We don't have much farther to go, do we? I don't remember it being so far away."

"It's not far. We're on the edge of the valley now. See how the plains darken? We are in red clay territory. That's how we know the difference. It shouldn't be long before we spot the hills. We'll find shelter there."

"I hope so. I've had all the sun I can handle." She looked over her shoulder. "Do you think the Black Guard is coming?"

Crane shrugged. "Eventually. But hopefully we'll be long gone before they arrive."

With the sun setting in the west and after hours of long riding, the hills of Crow Valley appeared in the distance.

Zora's breathing eased. For some reason, the rocky hills gave her a sense of security. She looked behind her and shielded her eyes. The long trek through the sun was over.

Razor allowed the wagon to catch up to him and rode beside Zora's side. "Welcome to the middle of nowhere. How quaint."

"You'll manage," Crane offered.

"What sort of people live in the rocks?" Razor asked as he shifted in his saddle. "There better not be a bunch of trolls, gnolls, goblins. That's what I've heard."

Crane leaned forward and looked past Zora. "It's a place where people go who want to be left alone. They won't ask questions unless we stay awhile, and even then, they might not say a word."

"Good," Razor said. "Sounds like a place where the ugly women live. Lucky me." He rode ahead.

"Some people have a one-track mind," Zora said.

"I think he has two tracks, women and fighting. But they often go together," Crane quipped.

"Have you checked the Medallion of Location recently?" she asked.

"Good idea. Why don't you fetch it for me? It's in my satchel."

Zora stretched over the bench and reached for the satchel. Dust devils formed on the trail behind her.

She squinted. *What is that?*

The dust devils scraped over the cracked earth, lifted into the sky, and vanished.

"Shew," she said, resuming her position in her chair.

"What?"

"Nothing. Dust devils. It spooked me." She fished the jewel box out of the satchel. "Here you go."

Crane checked behind him. "Dust devils. Hah. There are worse devils. That's for certain." He eyed the jewel box. "Go ahead. You open it."

Zora flipped open the lid and stared into the small inky void. Her eyes adjusted to the pitch-blackness as she shielded the box from the setting sun with her back. She gave it a few moments and said, "I don't see anything. Does that mean, you know?"

"Of course not. The medallion only gives a location, but in this case, not seeing the green spot is a good thing."

"It is?"

Crane nodded. "Absolutely. It means they're in Safe Haven. I can't detect anyone in Safe Haven. No one can," he said.

She gave him an incredulous look. "Where is this place? We should go there."

"We can't. It's not a place for ordinary mortals like us. We wouldn't survive the trip."

"So, you haven't been there?"

"I wouldn't want to go. There are monsters, as I under-stand it, big ones."

"Can you at least tell me where it is?"

Crane shook his head. "Nope."

The rest of the company formed a row and stopped ahead.

Crane brought the wagon to a stop between Jakoby and Gorva. "Is something the matter?"

Jakoby pointed at an object on the ground in their path ahead. It was very far away. "That."

"They're rocks. There will be lots of rocks from here on out," Crane said with a doubtful look. "You'll get used to it."

"Those rocks moved. I saw it," Gorva replied in her husky voice.

"There's a spyglass in my satchel. Fetch it, if you will," Crane said to Zora.

She handed him the spyglass. Crane extended the weathered spyglass and put it up to his eye. He shifted it from side to side. His mouth dropped open. "Dirty halfling. It can't be."

Zora snatched the spyglass and looked at the object. Ice raced down her spine. "Bloody horseshoes, that's Hella, isn't it?"

37

ZORA'S HEART pounded in her chest. There was no
mistaking Hella's evil countenance. She was everything the
Rogues of Rodden had described but worse. The Risker
leaned against her grand dragon's belly with a look of
supreme confidence on her face. She looked dead at Zora,
lifted up her fingers, and waved.

Zora's throat tightened. "It's her."

"Her who?" Jakoby took the spyglass from Zora's shaky
hand. "It's her and her dragon. A mighty big one at that."

"Let me see!" Razor reached for the spyglass and took it
from Jakoby. "It looks like I'm going to have to add killing a
dragon to my record. My, that's a big one. Look at those
eyes. They're bigger than my head. And that woman, goy,
she's a real beauty. Dark hair and dark eyes, I bet she'll
like me."

As the spyglass was passed around, Zora took out the dragon charm and locked her fingers around it. "We don't have anywhere to go, do we?" she asked Crane.

"We can't outrun a dragon. Not even in my wagon," he said.

Zora took a deep breath. "If anyone has any brilliant dragon-slaying ideas, now would be a good time to share them."

"The dragon is only half the problem," Jakoby said. "If it's true that she's a full-blooded natural, then we have two great enemies to contend with. And that's a veteran woman. I can see it in her eyes. She wields power, probably the wizard fire as well."

"And here we are without any wizards." Razor gave a hard nod. "Great!"

"Since when does a blade master rely on the aid of a wizard?" Jakoby asked.

"I don't need a wizard. I need a distraction." Razor waved his hands around in an arcane motion. "When their magic intertwines, I strike."

Jakoby huffed out a short laugh. "You're silly sometimes." He patted the long sword on his hip that he'd recovered from the Ruins of Thannis. "We have the gourn. They will serve us well. Fight dragon fire with dragon fire."

"Yeah, but gourn can't fly, can they? That dragon can turn us into kindling with one pass. What are we going to do then?" Razor asked as he patted down his weapons.

"Tell you what, I'll distract Hella with my charming nature, and you can take the dragon."

Gorva turned her horse and asked, "Speaking of charms, what about yours, Zora? Can you control that dragon?"

"I don't know. It's a grand, and she's a natural. Their bond will be difficult to break."

"Well, I suggest you'll find a way. It's the best hope we have," Gorva said as she handed the spyglass to Crane.

Looking through the glass, Crane said, "She's coming right toward us. She really has a strut about her. Those hips."

Zora snatched the spyglass. "She's going to kill us."

"I can think of worse ways to die," Crane admitted.

Razor leaned over his saddle horn and squinted. "Nice hips, you say? Enticing."

"Everyone who still has their tongues in their mouths and their brains in their skulls, listen," Zora began. "She wants to know about the Doom Riders and who killed them. We don't say a word about Grey Cloak, Anya, Dyphestive, or Cinder. We take that information to our graves, agreed?"

Everyone nodded.

"Good, now spread out. I'll let Crane do the talking," she finished.

With the wagon in the center, Gorva and Leena and their gourn moved to Crane's left and crept outward.

Jakoby and Razor did the same to Zora's right, making a half-circle formation. Razor was the only one of the four on horseback. The other horses were towed behind them.

"Buy us all the time you can," Zora said to Crane. "And don't flirt."

Crane gave her a surprised look. "That's my best way of making friends."

Hella boldly strode into the midst of the group. She stood empty-handed, sword on one hip and a whip on the other. She was tall for a woman, like Gorva, and very imposing in her dragon armor. "I am Hella the Risker, servant of Dark Mountain and general to Black Frost. You've probably heard of me."

"Nice to meet you in person," Crane said cheerfully. "I'm Crane. This is Zora, Gorva, Leena, Jakoby, and Reginald."

"Razor," Reginald corrected. "Reginald the Razor, and if you don't mind me saying so, I love your hair and cape."

Gorva scowled at him.

Hella didn't offer the blade master a glance. "Those gourn are very interesting mounts for people such as yourselves. I'd care to know how you came upon them."

"We acquired them on the road to the Iron Hills," Crane said. "The poor beasts were wandering, and we fed them."

Hella flashed her dark eyes. "Really? I'll have you know that these gourn are the personal property of Dark Mountain. We consider them stolen. Hence, you are all thieves, and the penalty for stealing a gourn is death."

"Uh..." Crane shrugged. "We didn't know."

Hella tilted her head to the side and gave him a doubtful look. "Come now. No ordinary man or woman would dare touch a gourn. They know they're the mounts of the Doom Riders, indentured servants of the mountain."

Gorva sat up in her saddle and stared the Risker down. "Finders keepers."

"You have a bold tongue. I like it. Perhaps I'll save your screams for mercy for last," Hella offered. "I am curious how you managed to subdue the beasts, given that the lot of you are so ordinary."

"I'm a Monarch Knight," Jakoby admitted. "We can ride any beast." He nodded to Gorva and Leena. "The same as them."

"You're telling me the woman with the bug on her face is a Monarch Knight? She looks like a monk to me." The corner of her mouth turned up into a smile. "Maybe she's a Monarch Monk. Of course, little is left of the Monarchy these days. They are merely puppets to contain civil unrest. The knights, of course, are useless. Most betrayed their oaths and joined the Black Guard."

Jakoby bristled. His hand drifted down to the pommel of his sword. "I would not say such things if I were you."

"Save your pride, knight." Hella approached the black nightmare, Vixen. She stroked the horse's nose. "This is a fine beast as well, a shiny coat, strong build, unique for pulling a large wagon that should be pulled by two beasts —or one large draft horse."

"She's a strong girl, and she's all I have," Crane said with a warm smile. "We are a team."

"I don't care about you or your horse. What I care about is information. I know you know who killed the Doom Riders, so don't play stupid. Tell me who it is." She drew her sword. "Or die."

38

ZORA KEPT HER EYES AVERTED, feigning fear and cowering in her cloak. What she was really doing was focusing on the dragon charm, summoning its power, and tapping into the mind of Hella's dragon. She could feel the dragon's mighty pulse in the palm of her hand, but his mind was as hard as stone. She sought an entrance.

"Listen, Hella, if you want to take these ugly horses back to the mountain, then so be it," Crane said. "You can have them, but leave us alone. We don't want any trouble with you or the Black Guard." He dabbed his face with a handkerchief. "Look, we're thieves. Nomads. Gypsies. Look at this motley group. Dirty and dusty. Can you blame us for seizing an opportunity?"

"Is that so?" Hella asked.

She cut her sword, pointed at the ground, from side to

side. It was a fine longsword with a one-sided grip and blade. The handle was pearl black and the metal hand-guard made from black iron. The blade shined against the sun.

"Why didn't you turn the gourn in for a reward?"

"If you'll permit my saying, it's not likely we would have made a profit from the Black Guard. If anything, we'd have been tossed in the dungeons. We felt our chances to make a profit would be best found in the south, where the Black Guard wouldn't bother us," Crane said.

Hella nodded. "I like you, Crane. You have a silky tongue. It amuses me." She rested her sword on her shoulder. "But this is how I see it. The Doom Riders were taking prisoners north when they came upon two dragons. The larger dragon killed Drysis the Dreadful."

"Who?" Crane asked.

Hella held up her hand. "The smaller, a middling, torched one of the other Doom Riders. The last two Doom Riders died in combat. Killing them would be no easy feat for a mere mortal. I can see that you have some worthy swords here, but you don't have dragons. That makes me suspicious. I want to know about these dragons."

"I swear to you, there weren't any dragons or people when we came upon them," Crane said. "Isn't it true that there are still dragons in the wild? A mother and child feeding perhaps?" he suggested.

"I ask a question, and you deflect by offering alternatives," Hella said with a frown. "It's tiresome. Do you know how many I have interrogated? Killed?" She patted her whip. "Brought under my lash? It doesn't bother me at all." She turned and looked back at her dragon. "I'm offering you a way out, a chance to clean the slate. Or I can end this quick and let my dragon, Steelhammer, burn you all to death." She looked at them. "What will it be? The truth or death and a prolonged interrogation of the chosen survivor?"

"I wish we had the answers that you seek, Hella. Please, take the gourn, and let us be on our way," Crane said.

"I'm going to give you a chance to come clean between now and when I return to my dragon." Hella walked backward. "If you don't surrender the truth before I arrive, we will kill not all but most of you." She sheathed her blade and started walking away. "The others will be interrogated until dead."

"Well, what are we waiting for?" Razor asked as he pulled two of his swords. "We can't let her get back to that dragon. We need to stop her now."

Jakoby shook his head. "We can't run her down, or the dragon will come at us." He looked at Zora and Crane. "What do we do?"

Crane put his hand on Zora's shoulder. "Tell me you can get control of that dragon."

"I'm trying, but his mind is a rock. I can't penetrate it."

She glanced up. Hella was halfway back to her mount. "Horseshoes."

"Concentrate, Zora. Concentrate. Controlling Hella's dragon is the only way out of this. Focus on one thing, one thing only," Crane urged.

"I am. I swear I am."

"You have to admit, Hella sure knows how to make an entrance and an exit. What a walk!" Razor said with a smile.

Jakoby nodded.

"What is wrong with you two?" Gorva asked.

"Sometimes you have to think happy thoughts, relax before a big fight." Razor twisted his swords in the air. "Why not, when you're about to die?"

Hella arrived at Steelhammer and climbed on his back. The grand dragon rose from his spot, spread his long wings, and let out a powerful roar.

"He's huge!" Razor said.

"For the Monarchy!" Jakoby added.

The dragon beat his wings. It lifted off the ground and rose into the air.

"Zora, we're going to be cooked. Concentrate. You can do this!" Crane said. He squeezed her hand. "I believe in you. We all do."

"I'm trying," she said desperately. Her heart pounded inside her chest. New sweat broke out on her brow. "But I feel nothing." She sobbed. "I'm sorry."

39

SWORDS SCRAPED out of their sheaths. Horses stamped their hooves and whinnied.

Zora could hear Razor say, "I wonder which ones of us she is going to kill. Remember, she didn't say all of us?"

Crane spoke to her, exhorting her, encouraging her. His words ran together. It was impossible to focus. Then Crane's words rang as clear as a bell. "We have faith in you. You have to have faith in you."

Zora lifted her gaze skyward. The dragon glided across the dusty landscape with silver fire in his eyes and fiery-hot breath building in his jaws. The terrifying monster blasted right over the group. They were hit by a hot blast of dust.

The dragon, Steelhammer, circled low to the ground. A geyser of flame shot out of his mouth, and he lit the ground on fire. A wall of flame burned before their wide eyes. The heat singed the hair on their skin.

Hella's commanding voice called on them. "Pray to the earth! Pray to the sky! Your day is over!"

The dragon pulled up, wings beating, creating a storm of dust. It turned in midair, flew away, and circled for another pass.

"Zora, you have to do this! That was only a warning! The next flames will consume us!" Crane said in a panic.

She stood in the wagon and lifted her arm high. She stared ahead, waiting to catch Steelhammer's eye.

The dragon finished his slow turn in midair and aimed for the company. Steelhammer's eyes passed over the group one by one. His stare was death, his breath fiery fury. He locked eyes with Zora.

She focused on a single thought. She searched for a crack into the great beast's mind. She revealed the dragon charm and hooked the dragon's gaze. Steelhammer's narrowed eyes widened. In his moment of doubt, Zora saw a way into his mind, and her single suggestion jumped from her mind into his. It was a soothing thought, a warm and fuzzy feeling, merely a suggestion. Not a forceful command. She snuck it in.

Sleep.

Fifty yards away and thirty feet high, Steelhammer's expansive wings went limp. Hella let out a startled cry. The dragon crashed to the ground with his eyes closed, pushing up dirt and skidding to a halt twenty yards from the company. Hella was catapulted between the dragon's horns and landed hard at the base of his nose.

The company of Talon exchanged dumbfounded looks.

As Hella started to rise, Jakoby said, "Surround her!"

From their mounts, Jakoby, Razor, Leena, and Gorva formed a tight circle around Hella.

Hella pulled her sword. She glared at Zora. "Oh, you're going to wish you didn't do that. I'll make you all pay!"

The Risker's words were a distant echo in Zora's mind. She focused on keeping Steelhammer asleep. The beast was restless, his will like iron. He fought her, mind against mind. He wanted to awaken. Stormy seas rose inside the beast.

I must calm him.

"Listen, Hella, natural or no natural, we have the advantage on you," Razor said with his manly charm. "And if you make one move, my friends are going to have their gourn roast you like a turtle in its shell."

"That's the dumbest thing I've ever heard," Hella said. "I think I'll kill you first." She leaned toward him.

Gorva poked her spear into Hella's chest and pushed her back. "He might be stupid, but you should still listen to the man."

"Do I look like someone who listens to anyone?" Hella asked. Her nostrils flared, and her chest expanded. "You're making a fatal mistake. Fatal!"

"Drop your sword, Hella," Jakoby ordered. "Or Gorva will run you through, and my gourn will flame you like roast on a spit."

Hella growled out loud with rage and stuck her sword in the ground.

"You aren't so tough without your dragon," Gorva mocked.

"Why don't you get off that gourn, put down that spear, and find out?" Hella suggested.

"Ladies, as much as I like a good catfight, we have more important matters at hand," Razor said. "Now that we have her, what do we do with her?"

"Tie her up," Jakoby said.

"I'd be happy to. Toss me some strips, Crane!" Razor said as he dismounted.

Crane tossed over a sack filled with strips of leather used for binding.

Razor caught it and approached Hella. With the air rife with tension, he coolly patted her down. He took the whip off first. "I don't think you'll be needing this." He found daggers hidden in her boots. "Or these, but I like the way you think." He patted her down one more time.

"Is this necessary?" Hella asked.

"I believe so, darlin'. A man like me can't take chances

with a dangerous woman like you. I know better." He grabbed her arm and tried to pull it behind her back.

She resisted. "Let go of me, dog!"

"Don't make this harder than it needs to be, Hella. Keep it simple. Be a good prisoner, and we'll get along fine." He wrenched her arms behind her back and tied them with leather cords. "There. That wasn't so bad, was it?"

"She's a natural. They have powers. Keep a close eye on her," said Jakoby. "If she so much as flinches, strike a blow to her temple."

"What are we going to do with her now?" Gorva asked.

Jakoby shrugged. "I don't know."

Steelhammer stirred. Zora broke out in a cold sweat and doubled over in the wagon. Crane caught her. Hella smiled.

40

Steelhammer's scales ruffled. His huge body shifted over the dirt. His head began to rise.

"Now might be the best time for you to surrender," Hella suggested. "Because Steelhammer is very moody when he wakes."

"Crane, what is going on?" Razor asked. He could see Zora slumped over in the older man's arms. "What's wrong with Zora?"

Exasperatedly, Crane said, "She passed out!"

"All of you are dead now, but I'll probably spare the two in the wagon," Hella said confidently.

Razor spun to say to her, "You're still our prisoner. And I'm sure your ugly pet won't harm us if we threaten to harm you."

"Look at my dragon. You don't stand a chance against

him, or me for that matter." Hella caught the group looking at the great beast. Her bracers came to life with wizard fire. The leather cords blackened and turned to ash.

"Razor, watch out!" Jakoby said.

The blade master turned right into a hard punch to the jaw that dropped him to a knee. In the wink of an eye, Hella snatched up her sword and whip. She batted Gorva's spear aside with her sword and caught Jakoby by the neck with her whip. She yanked him out of the saddle.

"Bloody biscuits, she's fast and sneaky!" Razor snaked his two longest blades out of their scabbards and rushed her. "May we dance?"

"Certainly," she replied.

He lunged, sword first. Hella twisted away and batted his sword aside. With a crack of her whip, she caught him by the ankle and jerked him off balance. Razor flopped onto his back. Her blade stabbed at his heart. He parried and thrust his other sword, sending her jumping backward.

A blossom of flames erupted from Gorva's gourn, consuming Hella for a moment. From out of nowhere, the Risker reappeared several feet away from the flames, where she stabbed the attacking gourn in the chest. The gourn tossed Gorva out of the saddle.

Razor climbed to his feet. Jakoby rose from the sand with a sword in his grip, spitting dirt from his mouth. Leena's nunchakus whirred in the air. They glowed with intensity. She set her eyes on Hella and attacked with both hands.

Clok! Clok! Clok! Clok!

Hella flailed away like she was being assaulted by a nest of angry hornets. She took hard shots to the face, the chin, her elbow, and shin. "Get away from me, gnat!" She sliced her sword at Leena.

Leena ducked under the woman's sword and side kicked her in the gut. She drummed on the woman's chest with her nunchakus.

Hella spun in her cape and skipped ten feet out of striking range in an instant.

"Whoa, you're full of surprises, aren't you?" Razor asked. "What's the matter? Can't you handle a straight fight?"

"Four against one isn't a straight fight, but if *you* want a straight fight, I'll give it to you." Hella waved her cape, vanished, and reappeared behind Razor's back. She stabbed him.

"Argh!" He jumped to one side at the last moment, avoiding a fatal blow.

Instead, she only sliced him in the side. Jakoby attacked with an overhead sword chop. Hella parried. Steel rang against steel. Their blades collided at the handguards.

The tall woman pushed back against Jakoby's great frame. "You will die today, knight. It is inevitable."

With a growl, Jakoby shoved her to the ground hard. He

pushed his full weight down on top of her. "We'll see about that!" He raised his fist. "What?" Hella was gone.

Razor slid in beside Jakoby and put pressure on his bleeding side. He helped Jakoby up. "She's going to be a problem."

Hella had faced off against Leena and Gorva. The women pinned their enemy between them and chased her down with nunchakus and a large spear.

Gorva thrust at Hella's belly, sending the woman darting away. "Stand still!"

Leena cut Hella off, dodged a crack of the whip, and kicked Hella in the face, drawing an angry scowl.

"Enough of this!" Hella shouted. Her sword and whip charged with wizard fire. Her eyes burned hot. Through clenched teeth, she said, "No more games!"

Gorva delivered a quick spear thrust. Hella hacked off the spear tip. With a flick of her wrist, she whipped Gorva around the neck. The shock of energy dropped Gorva to her knees. Gorva groaned, gave an angry snarl, grabbed the burning whip, and yanked it out of Hella's grip.

Leena sailed through the air in an aerial kick aimed for Hella's head.

Hella blinked out of sight and reappeared ten feet away from the company. With the sword still glowing in her hand, she said, "All this fighting and not a scratch on me." She looked at Razor. "How's your side, Reginald?"

"It's bleeding. Thanks for asking."

Behind the group, Steelhammer let out a snort of hot air. The restless dragon's eyes were still closed. His feet kicked, and his long serpentine tail swiped across the dusty land.

"She's buying time," Jakoby said as he eyeballed the dragon. "We have to take her down now if we're going to stand a chance." He whistled at his gourn. The dragon horse came to his side. "Perhaps they can help." He set his gaze on Hella. "Let's set her on fire. Attack!"

Jakoby's gourn charged forward with fire coming from its mouth and flames in its eyes. It bore down on Hella. She vanished and reappeared between two more attacking gourn. Flames burst out of their mouths, consuming her in a pillar of flame.

Razor shielded his eyes. The wroth heat warmed his face. "Is she gone?"

As quick as the flames started, they died down. The gourn clawed at the dry earth and sniffed it. Once again, Hella was gone.

"Where'd she go now?" Razor asked.

He felt the ground moving behind him. A tremendous shadow fell over the group. He turned all the way around, and the others joined him.

Steelhammer towered over the group.

Hella was seated on his back, and she glowered down at them. "Time to die, fools!"

41

CRANE STIFFLY SLAPPED Zora's cheek and gave her a firm shake. "Snap out of it, Zora!"

Zora gave him a lazy look. Her head ached, and she felt like she was moving underwater. "What happened?"

"You passed out." Crane hurried into the back of the wagon and cut the other horses loose.

Rubbing her head, she managed to sit up. She remembered suggesting that Steelhammer remain sleeping, but his durable will had proved too strong for her. He'd broken the charm and sent shards of pain coursing through her mind. "What's going on?"

"We're about to die. That's what's going on," Crane said as he jumped back into his seat. He grabbed her head and turned it. "Look!"

A few dozen yards away, Hella and Steelhammer were

poised to strike the other four members of Talon. The dragon swayed lazily and blinked his huge orb eyeballs.

Hella stood on his back screaming, "Torch them, Steel-hammer!" She kicked his horns. "What are you waiting for?"

Zora's sluggish mind snapped out of it. Her body awakened. "Thunderbolts, he'll burn them like kindling!"

"You think?" Crane cracked his lash. It sprouted with flames, and a glow ignited in his eyes. "There's only one way out of here. While that dragon's groggy, we need to head for the rocks. We have to buy all the time we can." He snapped the horsewhip across Vixen's back. Her eyes and hooves turned to flame. The wheels on the wagon ignited.

Vixen lunged forward, rocking the passengers backward. The wagon sped toward the company.

Zora waved her arm, yelling, "Get away from those gourn, and get in! Get in!" She still had the dragon charm in her grip. She fixed her attention on the gourn and pointed at Steelhammer. "Attack!"

The gourn raced at Steelhammer's body. They climbed all over him, clawing, biting, and unleashing hellish fire.

Razor and Gorva were the first to jump into the wagon. Jakoby and Leena stood their ground, weapons bared.

"Get in the wagon!" Zora shouted.

"No! We'll buy you more time!" Jakoby said. "Go!"

"Get in!" she yelled again. "Please!"

With his sword gripped in both hands, Jakoby said, "I've made up my mind. This is where I stand."

Zora felt the blood drain from her face when Leena gave her a simple nod.

"They've made up their minds. We have to go!" Crane said. "Yah, Vixen, yah!"

Steelhammer was making quick work of the gourn. His jaws bit down on one gourn and crushed it. Bones popped and snapped, and he flung the limp gourn's body aside.

Zora sat up in the wagon, looking back. The last thing she heard Jakoby say was, "Go for the wings. I'll handle Hella."

A javelin of fire came down from above, hurled by Hella. It pierced through Jakoby's shoulder and sent him to a knee.

"Noooooo!" Zora screamed with tears in her eyes. "Noooooo!" She tried to jump out of the wagon, but Gorva wrapped Zora up in her strong arms.

"There's nothing you can do now! Don't let their sacrifice be in vain!" Gorva squeezed. "We will avenge them. I swear it! We will avenge them all!"

The wagon of fire rocketed toward the hills. The distant battle faded. Dragon fire flashed over the field, scorching the ground. Several blasts set the world ablaze, and a pillar of smoke rose.

Zora sagged in Gorva's arms. "No, no, they didn't need to die." She sobbed.

"They died for what they believed in," Gorva said as she cradled Zora. "This is war. With war comes death, and it's not over yet."

"You can say that again," Razor said in his rugged voice. He beat on the side of the wagon. "Crane! I don't know where you're going, but you better get there soon! That dragon's coming!"

Far away, Steelhammer lifted off the ground and sped toward them.

"I don't know about you, but I think that dragon's flight isn't as smooth as it was. He's got a hitch!" Razor said. "They got a piece of him!"

Zora could see Steelhammer laboring to catch up, but the wagon still gained speed.

Vixen raced into the cover of the hills. The rocks blocked their pursuers from sight as they rumbled through the twists and turns of the jagged formations.

Zora wiped her eyes. "Crane, where are we going to go?"

"I'm hoping to find a hiding spot from that dragon. That's where. These hills are thick with caves, but if that dragon corners us, we'll be roast goose ready to serve at a holiday feast."

Vixen blasted through barren bushes and shrubbery and sliced over the rocky road like it was as smooth as glass. She traversed the slopes and hills like she'd been through a thousand times before while the others rode blind.

Zora held her stomach. She'd been slung around more than she cared for, and the pit in her stomach was about to empty.

"Hang on!" Crane drove the wagon through a hairpin turn that slung them all to one side. He had an elated expression on his face. "Fun, isn't it?"

Zora shook her head. She couldn't take her mind off the loss of Jakoby and Leena. She'd failed them.

The wagon jumped a gorge, crashed down on the other side, and raced up a steep incline.

"There!" Crane shouted. "There, Vixen!"

A cave opening big enough for the wagon waited for them on the hillside. Vixen pulled up alongside it. "Everyone in! Everyone in!" Crane looped his satchel over Zora's shoulder. "Hang on to this." He backed Vixen into the shadows in the mouth of the deep cave. "Everyone, stay quiet and relax. Take a breath." He eyed them all. "It might be the last one you get."

42

Roooooooaaaaar!

Steelhammer's dragon call echoed through the rocky hills, shaking the debris from the ceiling above.

"He sounds more wounded than angry," Razor said. He was just inside the rim of the cave, sword in hand, looking skyward. "But I don't see him."

The cave was large but not big enough for a grand dragon to fit inside. Zora and Gorva headed to the back. It kept going.

"It's deep, but 'How deep?' is the question."

Vixen's hooves and the wagon's wheels had cooled.

Crane hollered back at them, "What did you find?"

"There's a passage, but we don't know how far it goes or if it will protect us from dragon fire!" Gorva hollered back. "We might be stuck in a chimney, for all I know."

Zora's hands were shaking.

Gorva put her hand on Zora's back. "Take a deep breath."

"I'm trying. I can't, and my heart's beating in my ears."

"Don't fall apart on us now. You've done well so far." Gorva rubbed Zora's back. "Can you use the charm again?"

Zora shook her head. "No. He's too strong, and he'll be ready for it." She fingered the Scarf of Shadows. "If I could only hide us all with this."

Gorva gave her a straight-faced look. "You might have to save yourself. It might be the only way for any of us to survive."

Razor shuffled deeper into the cave, holding his side. "A giant shadow went overhead. That dragon is getting close. Can he smell us?"

Crane shook his head. "One thing about Vixen's powers is that her fires don't burn a trail. They cover our tracks." He looked deep in the passage and rubbed his open jaw. "I don't think the wagon will roll down there. All of you, go and explore. I have to unhitch Vixen."

Rooooooooaaaaaaar!

The sound was closer that time.

"Flaming Fences, I felt that one," Razor said. He lumbered deeper into the cave. "Hurry it up, Crane."

"Coming!" Crane replied.

Zora peered forward. "We need a light."

"If we don't get moving, we're going to have more light

than we're ever going to need," Razor said. "Hurry it up, Crane!"

Wupash!

Zora spun around on her heel at the sound of the cracking whip. Vixen's hooves and the wagon's wheels caught fire. Crane was standing on the bench of the wagon with fire in his eyes.

"Goodbye, everyone! I hope I see you again." He cracked the flaming lash over the horse's back. "Eeyah! Here comes the Flaming Thunder, dragon!"

Vixen and the wagon jumped out of the cave and vanished down the slope.

Zora ran after them, screaming, "Craaane! Craaane!"

Gorva tackled her before she made it out of the cavern.

She kicked Gorva in the gut. "Get off me!"

Gorva pulled her down like a child. "Don't be a fool! Crane knows what he's doing."

All three of them stood in the mouth of the cave watching the dimming skies. The wind picked up, and sandy grit got in their eyes.

"A storm is coming," Gorva murmured.

Zora could hear dragon wings beating. She gasped.

Suddenly, Steelhammer and Hella dropped out of the sky and hovered in the air. The dragon's wings fought hard to keep him afloat. Part of one wing was ripped open in several places.

"I will find you!" Hella called out in a booming voice. "I will destroy you the same as the others!"

From their lofty position, Steelhammer and Hella scanned the crooked channels. The dragon started to pivot in midair. The dragon and rider locked their eyes on the cave at the same time. Hella licked her teeth. Zora's heart jumped. Steelhammer's roar shook the air. Fire built up behind the scales of his breast.

"Finish this!" Hella ordered.

"Wooooo-hoooooooo!" someone shouted in a familiar voice from above the swirling winds.

Steelhammer and Hella's eyes widened as their heads whipped around.

Vixen charged up a steep incline, snorting fire with flames in her eyes. The entire wagon, Crane and all, became a torpedo of flame. They launched into the sky fifty feet and slammed into Steelhammer's chest like a flaming battering ram.

There was a resounding collision, a great ball of fire. The dragon squealed. A woman screamed. The mangled heap of wood, wheels, scales, and claws plummeted downward and crashed beyond the rocks into the twisting teeth of the channels below.

"Did that happen?" Gorva asked, blinking.

The wind continued to pick up and whistle through the hills.

"Gooseberries, that did." Razor's shock was erased by a slight smile. "And it was unbelievable!"

The winds grew so strong that Zora covered her eyes. "We have to help them!" The sky turned pitch-black. She couldn't see ten feet out of the cave. "Come on!"

Gorva held her back. "I'm sorry, but we aren't going anywhere. That sandstorm will suffocate us all. It's safest here."

"How can you stand here and watch our friends die?" she shouted. "I'm the leader! Listen to me!"

Gorva and Razor gave her a sorrowful look.

He nodded, winced, and said, "If you insist, we'll go." He put his head down and started out of the cave. The sand covered him up, and the wind knocked him over.

Zora grabbed his arm and hauled him back in. "No, we'll stay," she said with a look of defeat. "We'll stay."

43

ZORA AND GORVA ventured as deep as the cave would allow while Razor remained behind and rested. The sandstorm hadn't shown any signs of letting up, leaving them in near-total darkness. But inside Crane's satchel, Zora found a candle that would light by simply blowing on it. Crane had mentioned it to her before, and she would have all but forgotten about it if she hadn't rummaged through his satchel in desperation.

"There isn't even a cave bat inside here," Gorva said as she stood at the dead end, inspecting the rocks. "And it's not nearly as deep as we hoped for either. Certainly, that dragon would have turned our skins to ash."

Zora moved the candle back and forth and raised it up higher. Some of the rocks in the ceiling glinted, and there was a large cleft above her head. "We still had a card to play. She didn't want all of us dead. She wants information. We had that."

Gorva nodded. "True."

Zora's shoulders sagged, and she sat down and leaned back against the wall. "I can't believe they're gone."

"Me either." Gorva took a seat beside her. "But we're still alive because of them. I don't believe we would have made it any other way. Don't doubt yourself now. You make good decisions."

It took everything Zora had not to break out in tears. The lump in her throat swelled, and her eyes watered. "Here," she said quietly. She handed Gorva the candle and covered her face in her hands. Her friends were gone, and she would never see them again. It hit her hard.

Gorva cradled Zora under her long arm like a child. "It's hard to lose friends. I know. I lost all of my family to the evil of Black Frost."

"I'm so sorry." She sniffed. "I'm tired of people dying. Well, except for those Doom Riders. They killed Browning, Dalsay, and Adanadel back when all of this started. Now, thanks to Black Frost, Leena, Jakoby, and Crane are gone as well. It hurts. I can't imagine how it feels to lose your family."

"It hurts, too, but it also keeps me alive. If we don't stop these monsters, more people will suffer and die."

"I know," she said softly. She wiped her tears on her trousers and stood back up. Taking a quick breath, she said, "Boost me up. I want to see what's inside that fissure."

"Easy enough." Gorva handed Zora the candle and boosted her up by the waist as if she were a baby.

Using the candle, Zora had a full view inside the cleft, but the light faded into the darkness. "I think I can crawl in, but there's a rock in the way." She pushed it.

The rock moved. An orange eye opened a slit. Jaws opened, baring hundreds of razor-sharp teeth. The lizard struck.

Zora jerked her hand away just before the cave lizard could take it off. "Lizard! Lizard!" She twisted out of Gorva's grasp and fell to the ground.

The candle slipped from her fingers and went out. Gorva let out a painful shout. Two figures thrashed in the darkness. A tail swatted Zora across the face like a huge whip. It twisted her around.

In the dark, the figures slammed into the walls, the ground. Cries of pain and screeches echoed. Grunting and hissing combined with heavy bodies thudding against the stone.

Zora's fingers raked over the ground, searching for the candle. She called out, "Gorva! Gorva!"

The loud sound of flesh and bone popping and tearing was followed by a savage yell.

Crack!

Zora's fingers wrapped around the candle. She blew it. A flame ignited. She gasped.

Gorva sat on the ground panting. She was scratched all over and bleeding. A cave lizard more than half as big as her lay across her lap. It was a nasty black thing with claws and teeth as sharp as knives. Its head was twisted upside down. A long black tongue hung out of its mouth.

Zora looked into the whites of Gorva's eyes. "Are you well?"

Gorva nodded. "I've been scratched worse than this."

"What's going on down there?" Razor shouted.

The women responded in tandem, "Nothing."

"Didn't sound like nothing." Razor's tired face entered the radius of candlelight. "Did you find anything?"

Gorva shoved the lizard off her lap. "Nothing but dinner."

"Ew. Well, if that's all you found, you might as well come back this way. The storm has passed."

Sand had built up almost head high outside the cave. The three of them waded through it until they made it to their feet and climbed. Every nook and cranny of the hills were covered in sand, and night had fallen. It was pitch-black underneath the bed of stars. The shadows in the rocks made it worse.

Zora didn't hear any dragon calls. Aside from the wind

whistling through the rocks, she heard nothing at all but the soft sound of footsteps on sand.

Razor kept his voice down and asked, "So, where are we headed exactly?"

"We need to look for Crane," Zora said.

"I don't think Crane is coming back, and we don't know for certain that Hella and her dragon have perished. If they haven't perished, they'll still be looking for us," Razor said.

Zora kept going in the direction of where she'd watched Crane and Vixen fall. If there was a chance that they'd survived, she was going to help him. And if Hella and Steel-hammer had survived, Zora and her remaining companions were probably dead anyway.

"I go where you go," Razor said. "Lead the way."

They navigated the sandy terrain through the channels of rock only to find themselves crisscrossing through their own tracks. One wall of rock looked the same as another. The side of the ridge where Crane had fallen proved more challenging to find when navigating through a maze of rock.

After the remaining Talon members had walked for hours, a new day began, and Zora climbed the rocks and got a better look at the terrain. A channel led into an open field of sand, and she could see a wagon wheel jutting out of the ground.

"I see it! Get up here!"

Razor shook his head. "I have to climb? I hate climbing."

Zora climbed down the rocks into the channel and ran full speed, sand flipping up behind her heels, until she made it to the wagon wheels. She started digging with her hands. "Crane! Crane!"

44

THE TRIO DUG a wagon wheel deep and started digging away at the side.

That was when Gorva pulled the wheel out of the ground. She gave it a curious look. "I don't think this is the same wheel as Crane's wagon had. The spokes are a different make, more similar to what I've seen on chariots."

Zora dusted the sand from her hands. She had sand in her hair and boots. It was everywhere. "I could have sworn this was the spot."

"I don't think it was," Razor said, scratching his head. "The sandstorm filled this bowl about three feet or so, but if this were the spot, we'd have to see more of Crane's wagon and the dragon, and I don't see no dragon. Maybe the storm scared them off."

Zora knelt, at a total loss. Crane and Vixen had vanished into thin air. There was no wagon, no wreckage.

"Perhaps when he became a fireball, it destroyed them. Maybe it destroyed the Risker too," Gorva suggested. She flipped the wheel away. It rolled across the sand and fell over. "I've heard stories of men with strange powers who can bring total destruction. It's their death call. Crane was an odd man. It wouldn't surprise me if he had such powers."

"That sounds like a good explanation to me. I say we count our blessings and move on," Razor said as he dumped sand from his boots. "And with the wagon gone, we'll need water soon. We need to find a well or river, or we'll cook out here."

With effort, Zora pushed herself up to her feet. She was exhausted, and it took everything she had to keep her head up. As she scanned the area, she cradled Crane's satchel, hoping to see some sign of him. The fact that he'd vanished left her empty.

"Come on," Gorva said as she towed Zora along. "Don't think so hard about it. Not everything that happens has an explanation we can comprehend. You need to believe that Crane cleared a safe path for us. We need to find food and shelter, or we will become nothing but dry bones."

Zora gave a defeated nod and trudged south with her friends. They stayed close to the hills, walking in the shadows, avoiding the sun wherever they could. Zora's body felt like it was filled with sand. The entire trek and the battles had drained her. The fire in her was gone.

"As much as I yearn for ale, I'd settle for a warm glass of water now." Razor cracked his neck from side to side. "Why in Gapoli would Crane have us come into this godsforsaken land? Nothing's here. I haven't even seen a horned lizard. Well, aside from that dragon."

"You seem to have enough spit in your mouth to talk," said Gorva. "Maybe you aren't as thirsty as you think you are."

"Heh. Aren't you the witty one? Stone-faced and funny. I guess that's why you were Crane's chosen."

Gorva shot him a look. "What do you mean chosen? I am no man's woman."

"Well, we made a deal. He'd marry you, and I'd marry Zora. I guess now that he's gone, I'll have to take care of you both," Razor added a smile.

"We can take care of ourselves. Look at you, gimpy," Gorva said.

"I'm not gimpy. A little sore is all. And look at you with all those scratch marks on you. You're in worse shape than I am."

"Am not. You can barely walk."

Razor lengthened his stride and passed Gorva. "Eat my sand."

The pair raced ahead.

Zora paid them little mind. Her thoughts were elsewhere. She wrestled with her decisions. *I shouldn't have let Crane decide. If we'd gone to Dwarf Skull, we'd be safe by now.*

It was awful thinking bad thoughts about a dead man, but Crane's judgment had become suspect. She'd trusted it, and that had gotten most of them killed. Perhaps the remaining three would die as well.

Gorva and Razor vanished around the next bend in the rocks. Their bickering vanished with them.

The quiet wind offered the comfort Zora needed as it rustled her hair and cooled the sweat on her face. She forged ahead with her feet burning like hot coals inside her boots. Something had given her a new sense of determination, as if the wind had lifted her spirits.

A small shadow crossed her path and disappeared in the rocks. She looked up. At first, she thought it was a dragon, but upon a closer look, she saw three birds of prey circling. They were little more than black images in the sky, but her keen vision made out their feathery wings.

Thank the Monarchs. She made a head tilt. *Wait a moment. If they're circling, there might be a dead body ahead.*

She hurried around the next bend in the rock. Another channel sloped downward, but Gorva and Razor had vanished.

No!

Zora took off at a full sprint. She quickly came upon another bend in the path and rushed by it.

A strong arm hooked hers. A firm hand clamped over

her mouth before she could scream. She noticed Razor hiding in the rocks off to the side and immediately realized that Gorva had secured her.

"Shhhhh," Gorva murmured in her ear. Her hand slid away from Zora's mouth, and she pointed with her finger.

Ahead, in a small gorge, lay the body of Steelhammer with Hella resting by his side.

45

HELLA'S EYES WERE CLOSED, and her hands were empty. She lay against Steelhammer in an awkward position. The dragon's scales were scorched by fire, and his broken wings were collapsed on his back. Neither one of them moved.

The trio was still far enough away where they could speak in whispers.

Razor said, "I think they're dead." He slid a sword out of his scabbard and handed it to Gorva. "But I'm not taking any chances." He inched forward.

"Wait, what are you doing?" Zora asked.

"Finishing the job if it isn't finished," he replied.

"We need to leave well enough alone. We'll go elsewhere." Zora looked closer. She saw no sign of Crane, Vixen, or the wagon. "They must have moved during or after the storm, which means they must have been alive to do it."

"Or they crashed again," Gorva said. "Zora, I agree with him. We need to make sure this is done. Hella won't get the drop on us, not like that."

"I think everyone has made enough sacrifices. It needs to stop now. We need to move on."

"If Hella and that dragon aren't dead, they'll come after us." Razor drew a smaller blade from his chest. "We can't risk being caught in the open."

"Look at that dragon. It can't fly. How will she catch us?" replied Zora.

"She's a natural. You never know, and she won't give up the hunt." He eased out of the shadows and approached.

"I'm going with him. This is the best chance we have to secure our safety. We can't hesitate." Gorva stole away from Zora and caught up with Razor.

Zora watched them approach the enemy. She was on pins and needles. In her mind, she envisioned Steelhammer coming to life and consuming them both in a waterfall of flame. She reached inside the satchel and grabbed the dragon charm. Doubtful it could still help, she still felt a small measure of security from holding it.

Gorva's and Razor's footfalls were as silent as cats' feet as they walked over the soft bed of storm sand. They split apart several feet away and flanked Hella.

If the Risker was breathing, Zora couldn't tell. She saw

no gentle rise and fall of her chest. She didn't twitch a finger or flicker a lash.

Zora rose up on her toes and moved to a closer spot. Gorva's broad shoulders blocked her view of Hella. *Goy!*

Razor stood ten feet away from Hella. He gave Gorva a look, and she readied her sword and returned a nod. With his fingers tingling, he took a breath and shuffled closer. He bent at the knees and stretched his sword out at what appeared to be a vanquished woman. Keeping his eyes on Hella's, he poked her dragon armor covering her ribs. The flexible gear was made of small plates of hard steel designed to resemble a dragon's scales. When she didn't move, he nudged her harder.

Hella didn't budge. Razor glanced at Gorva and shrugged. Gorva's heavy stare remained fixed on Hella. Her wary gaze didn't change. She gave Razor the throat-slashing hand signal. Razor shook his head.

Gorva traced her finger over the skin of her forearm and looked at Hella. She mouthed the words, "Have you ever seen a dead body with skin like that before?"

Hella's deeply tanned skin was as healthy as any woman basking in the sun. Her jaw didn't hang open in a loose position either. Razor had seen the dead before, and none of them had ever looked as good as Hella, but he wasn't going to kill her in cold blood. He silently spoke back. "I don't kill like that. You do it."

Sword poised to strike a lethal blow, Gorva went in for the kill.

Hella's eyes snapped open. Tendrils of lightning erupted from her fingertips and pierced through Gorva and Razor's bodies. The spidery strands of energy lifted the pair from their feet. Their blades fell from their fingers. They spasmed in midair.

"The fool who hesitates is dead," Hella gloated as she came to her feet and cut off the wizard fire.

Gorva and Razor dropped to the ground and writhed in the sand. Their fingers curled into their palms, and they kicked their feet.

Hella calmly picked up a fallen sword and strolled over to Gorva. She lifted the orc's head up by her braids. "You were going to kill me in my sleep. Perhaps I'll give you the same pleasure you were determined to give me?" She put the blade to Gorva's throat.

"No!" Razor pleaded as he fought his way to his hands and knees. "K-Kill me, please, not her."

"Oh, a noble sacrifice. How delicious is that?" Hella stuffed Gorva's face in the sand, stood, and kicked her in the ribs with her steel-toed boots. "Why not? I'll kill you and make her watch. Steelhammer! Wake up! Playing possum is over!"

The mangled and charred form of the dragon stirred in

the sand. Steelhammer groaned and gasped a hot breath. He wheezed when he spoke. "Let me eat them. I hunger."

"I need one of them alive for information." Hella looked between the two heroes. "Wasn't there a third one with a dragon charm? Where is she hiding?" A blade burst out of the front of Hella's chest. Her face paled like snow. "Urk!"

"I'm right behind you, witch!" Zora said as she reappeared with the Scarf of Shadows covering her nose. "That's for my friends. Enjoy your time behind the Flaming Fence!" She shoved Hella to the ground.

Razor took a knee and grunted. "A fine job, but what about him?"

Zora turned and faced the battered, monstrous, and angry form of Steelhammer.

46

STEELHAMMER'S huge eyes burned like molten silver. His gaze and hot breath swept over the three of them. "Pesky creatures. Always trying to overachieve. You've sealed your deaths now."

Zora held her ground and raised the glowing dragon charm before Steelhammer's eyes. "Stay back," she ordered.

The dragon's laughter mimicked the sound of rolling thunder. "That bauble tricked me once, flea. It won't *ever* happen again."

Steelhammer was huge. His head was bigger than the three of them put together. Zora drew her shoulders back and repeated, "Stay back!"

The grand dragon returned a spacy stare. His horns and head tilted over. The fiery glow behind his chest cooled.

His body remained as still as a stone as he stared at the dragon charm.

"Get back," Zora murmured to her friends. "Hurry."

Gorva and Razor slow-walked backward.

Zora kept her concentration and walked with them. Out of the corner of her eye, she caught a sudden movement.

Steelhammer's tail swept their feet out from under them. They were tossed head over heels and landed flat on their backs. His tail went up and down, clubbing Gorva and Razor into the ground.

Zora shook her head as she struggled to stand. She saw the dragon charm half-buried and glinting in the sand. She reached for it.

Steelhammer closed in and snatched her in his front claws. "No you don't, pest." His hot breath seared her face. "Today, I feast on your little bones."

A sharp whistle sounded in the air, followed by loud popping and explosions.

"Roooooooaaaaar!" Steelhammer let out an angry howl. He dropped Zora and twisted his head over his back.

Boom! Boom! Boom!

Great birds dropped balls of black pitch from the sky. It splattered and coated the dragon's wings. Glowing spheres of energy followed and blasted into the dragon's body.

Zora scrambled over the sand as the entire chaotic scene exploded.

Steelhammer was being attacked by a flock of humongous vultures with small riders on their backs. Three of the vultures landed on the ground. They were as big as middling dragons.

A bearded gnome, as bald as an egg, with human-sized hands and big bulging eyeballs, waved to Zora. In a peppy voice, he said, "Get on! Get on!"

Zora snatched up the dragon charm and sprinted for the giant vulture.

"Hurry! Hurry!" the little vulture rider pleaded.

Steelhammer's angry roars could be heard across the entire territory as he was peppered with black pitch and energy balls.

Zora climbed into the saddle behind the gnome. Gorva and Razor were still down on the ground. "Pick them up! Pick them up!" she said.

Two more giant vultures dropped from the sky and snatched the knocked-out fighters in their claws. They lifted into the air, wings beating hard and picking up speed.

The giant vultures were ugly birds covered in ebony feathers up to their bare necks. They were as bald as their gnome riders but nasty looking with ugly beaks.

They rose higher and higher into the air. Steelhammer's bellows faded. His body vanished behind the rocks.

Zora saw nothing but safety and open sky. "Thank you," Zora said as she studied the flock of vultures. They were unlike any creatures she'd ever seen, and the gnomes were truly different. They were all dressed in primitive leather, skins, and feathers. She spoke into the gnome's pointed ear. "Who are you?"

"I am Durmost! And you're welcome!" He appeared older but was strong voiced. His skin was tan and leathery. "We are called the Southern Storm!" He cackled. "We rule the skies down here."

She placed her hands on his little shoulders. "No offense, but I've never heard of you."

"It's best that we are forgotten! That's how we want it!" He looked at her and smiled. "What's your name?"

"Zora!" She had to raise her voice to speak above the wind.

"You attract a great deal of trouble, Zora! You brought a dragon to our parts, didn't you?"

"In a matter of speaking. I'm sorry about that!"

"No, don't be sorry. We're glad you came along when you did. We spied the dragon and his rider playing dead, and we weren't sure until you sprung their trap." Durmost cackled. "It's been decades since we've had excitement like that. Our leader keeps us from the trouble of the north."

"You aren't the leader?" she asked.

"Only of this pack of sky gnomes and many more I might add," he said proudly. "I'm taking you to our home. It's not far away. You'll be safe there."

"No offense, but we can't stay long. We're on a mission."

"Maybe so, but you'll need rest. Refreshments! And my

leader will insist on meeting the persons who we risked our lives for and why." He petted her hand with his hand, which was surprisingly bigger than hers. "Don't be nervous. Our leader is wise! Our leader is kind!"

Flying nearby, in the *V* formation, Gorva and Razor hung lifeless in the claws of the great vultures. *I pray they are well.*

With the wind whistling through her ears, Zora allowed herself to enjoy the comfort of the sky.

"It's peaceful up here, isn't it?" Durmost asked. "There's no place in the world like the warm winds of the south caressing your face! Rest, dear, rest! You are safe with the sky gnomes. That's the promise of Durmost the sky gnome!"

Zora's eyes became heavy, and soon she fell asleep.

47

SAFE HAVEN

DYPHESTIVE WALKED the picturesque caverns alone. He saw plants that he'd never seen before—patches of flowers that shined like coins, mosses that were thick and soft like sponges. Strange albino bats with bright-pink eyes hung from the ceiling over the small lakes with fresh, ice-cold water.

He knelt down and scooped a handful of water and drank. He took a deep breath through his nostrils. "Ahhh... this is better." He lay back on a pillowy floor of orange moss and closed his eyes.

Safe Haven was quiet. He needed quiet.

Over the last few days, there had been a lot of excitement as well as bickering while getting to know the dragons. Grey Cloak and Anya were going at it regarding how to attack Black Frost. Grey Cloak remained focused on using the Figurine of Heroes to oust the underlings. Anya wanted no part of the Wizard Watch or their vile towers, as she called them. She wanted to start chipping away at Black Frost's forces.

With Dyphestive, there was little to question. He leaned with his brother. He always did, and he would now. But the bickering had become a bit much, as one party seemed as obsessed as the other with their ideas, and nothing was being compromised. Dyphestive decided it was time for a long walk.

He'd become fascinated by the trio of grand dragons, Rock, Smash, and Snags. As quickly as they'd appeared for an introduction, all of them had vanished. He'd been searching for them, and so far, he hadn't had any luck.

How can creatures so large hide so well?

According to Anya, the caverns went on for leagues. The dragons could be anywhere. It might take him weeks to find them, if he found them at all, but it gave him something to do.

His heavy limbs eased deeper into the moss, and he felt himself drifting back and forth between sleep and consciousness. At the moment, he was so comfortable that he didn't have a care in the world. He breathed deeply in a totally relaxed state and let the comfort of Safe Haven take him in.

Dyphestive awakened feeling refreshed from head to toe. His body was as warm as a hot roll. *Ah, this is wonderful.* His lids were caked shut with eye crust that he started to clean away. He reached over and hit something as hard as stone. *Huh?* He pushed up at the heavy object that didn't budge.

Dyphestive rubbed the grit from his eyes with his fists. "Gah!" He sat up quickly and bonked his head on the rock that hung over him. He rolled out of the bed of moss, which ripped from the floor's surface and clung to his body like glue. He found himself face-to-face with a dragon. It was the massive, brawny form of Rock.

"You!" he said, exasperated. "Don't you know better than to sneak up like that on someone sleeping?"

"No. This is our grazing field," answered Rock. "And you snore so loud it disturbed us. We thought a cave troll had entered our domain."

"I don't snore." Dyphestive started picking the orange moss from his shoulders. "This sticks to me like it would to a rock."

"You snore like a cave troll." Rock turned. His tail forced Dyphestive to duck out of the way. "Worse than a cave troll."

"I don't snore worse than a cave troll."

"So now you're admitting you snore? We've made progress." Rock made his way down the slope and started to drink from a freshwater lake. Smash and Snags were wading in the same waters.

"I'm not admitting anything."

A cackle caught his ear. He turned and saw Nath sitting nearby with his arms locked around his knees.

"You've made new friends," Nath said as he rocked back and forth like a curious child. "Take my advice, and don't tick them off."

"Why would I do that?" he asked in frustration as he continued to pick the moss from his body. "Only a fool would upset a dragon."

"You are wise, young fella." Nath wiped his stringy hair from his eyes and rose. "Turn around." He cleared the moss from Dyphestive's back. "You are fortunate that the moss didn't overtake you. A week longer, and you would have suffocated."

"Really? A week longer? How long have I been asleep?"

"A week or so."

"A week!"

Rock lifted his head from the waters. "And you've been snoring the entire time too."

"Are you serious, Nath?"

The imposing hermit nodded.

"Why didn't someone wake me?"

"No one was going anywhere, not at the rate Grey Cloak and Anya are going. They aren't speaking now. It's been a few days." Nath moved away to a patch of forest-green mushrooms that stood knee-high. He ripped one out by the roots, filling his arms. He handed it to Dyphestive.

"What's this?"

Nath nodded to Rock. "Take it to him. They like these."

Dyphestive gave Nath a funny look and shrugged an eyebrow. "If you say so." He strolled down the slope and stood by Rock. "Ahem."

Without lifting his snout from the water, Rock stared at him.

In the middle of the lake, Snags and Smash spit water and sprayed each other. They sent waves of water rolling over the bank.

"Rock, would you like a mushroom?" Dyphestive asked.

"I can feed myself."

Dyphestive gave Nath a disappointed look. Using his hands, Nath urged him on.

"I hear these are really good." Dyphestive tilted the mushroom back and forth in an enticing fashion. "They make your body strong, your scales as hard as iron."

"Sure." Rock swung his head around. "Fine, if it amuses you, feed me." He lowered his head to the ground and opened his huge mouth, which was more than big enough for Dyphestive to fit inside. He had thousands of teeth, large and small, and most of them as sharp as knives.

Dyphestive tossed the mushroom inside and stepped away.

Without chewing, Rock swallowed it whole. "Are you happy now?" He returned to drinking from the lake.

Disappointed, Dyphestive trudged up the slope toward Nath and stopped in front of him. "What was the point of that? I feel like an idiot."

Nath grinned. "No, you aren't an idiot, but that was funny."

48

CINDER CONVENED a small council of dragons, which included the Triplets, Feather, Fenora, and Streak along with Grey Cloak. Anya had stormed off since the last heated discussion and hadn't been seen since.

Grey Cloak stood beside Feather, twirling the Rod of Weapons with one hand. Much like the Cloak of Legends, he'd become comfortable having it in hand. It gave him an ability to control his wizard fire. He'd even been able to master turning the energy into a blade as well as a spear tip.

"Father, we're ready to fight. I say that we go with Anya," Fenora said. She towered over everyone but her father. "And I like the plan." She glanced down at Grey Cloak. "No offense, but I don't understand why we need to be bonded with the races anyway. Black Frost is a dragon, and he's the problem."

"As independent as we are, we have to work with the people of this world. This is how it has always been. We protect them, and they watch out for us," Cinder said. "It is a special bond and a good one when used for the right purposes."

"But they're tiny. We are big," Fenora objected.

"And Black Frost is bigger than all of us, bigger than the giants. You need to trust that we need one another for our own survival. It's the way of life on this world," Cinder added.

"If you say so." Fenora sighed and walked away. "I think I'll go look for Anya."

"Don't be offended, Grey Cloak. Fenora is a feisty one," Feather said. She stretched out her wing and touched his shoulder. "Grey Cloak?"

He'd been lost in his own thoughts. "Huh? Oh, sorry. What were we talking about?"

Feather sighed. "Nothing that we hadn't discussed before."

"Sorry." He squeezed the claw on the end of her wing. "My mind is wrestling with a problem that I ran into earlier." A blade of energy that had blossomed on the top of his rod vanished. "Aside from Cinder, have any of you met me before? Be honest. Now is not the time for secrets."

The Triplets, nestled at Cinder's feet, shook their heads. Feather and Cinder offered him a confused look.

"I thought so," Grey Cloak said with disappointment.

"Please explain," Cinder requested.

Grey Cloak set his staff to the side and sat down on a giant toadstool. "I found everything I needed in the Ruins of Thannis, but most importantly, the Figurine of Heroes. It was as if I'd put it there. I mean, we were trapped once we got there, but we had everything we needed to get back out. It wouldn't have been possible unless I'd been there before." He smirked. "I know it sounds crazy."

"I like crazy. Keep going," Feather suggested.

"There were dead people, people from Talon, or at least it looked like their bones and equipment. I could see it as plain as day. It was them. I felt a chill go through me. But there they were, with me, alive and well—and dead. I think some of us died in Thannis before, but we ended up having to go back again."

Feather looked up at her father. "Does that make any sense to you?"

"There is much in this world that even I don't understand," Cinder said. "My focus has always been serving the Sky Riders."

"Continue. This is exciting," Feather said.

"Indeed," Streak added.

Grey Cloak's face warmed. They didn't think he was the fool that he thought he was. "I believe I might have used the portal, or the Time Mural, in the Wizard Watch at another place in time. I can't explain it because what happened the first time was random, but that's the only way I can figure how we survived Thannis."

"I believe it." Streak's pink tongue flickered out of his mouth. "I went through it, too, and strange things happened. But, hey." He shrugged his wings. "I'd do it again if I had to."

"What are you getting at, Grey Cloak?" Cinder asked.

"I think we can use the Time Mural to stop Black Frost."

"What you say is madness."

Grey Cloak looked up and found Anya squatted on rocks nearby. Her arms were locked around her knees.

"I thought you ran away."

"I snuck back because I couldn't resist your foolish babbling." Anya jumped down and landed across from him. "You don't have any way of controlling time. Quit filling their minds with delusions."

Grey Cloak's jaw tightened. He gave her a cross look. "I'm not trying to control time, and the Time Mural isn't a delusion. I've been through it."

"And you had no control over where you went!"

"No, not ten years ago, but if the underlings and Black Frost learn to control it, think of the power they'll wield. They'll be able to destroy anyone and anything. That's why we have to go to Arrowwood and put a stop to them." He firmly tapped his index finger to his head. "Can't you get that through your thick skull? We can't beat Black Frost with force. We have to outmaneuver him."

Dyphestive and Nath showed up.

"I see nothing has changed since we left." Dyphestive gave Grey Cloak and Anya a disappointed look. "What are we arguing about this time?"

With their fists balled at their sides, the irritated elf and the woman answered in unison, "The Time Mural!"

49

"Whew, I can feel the steam coming off these two," Feather said. "One's as hardheaded as the other."

"Watch it, Feather," warned Anya. Her arms were crossed at her waist, and she turned her back to Grey Cloak. Her foot tapped the ground. "Go ahead and do what you want, Grey Cloak. That's what you're best at."

"Well, if that isn't the pot calling the kettle black." He shook his head and noticed his brother's disappointed expression. "What?"

"Anya." Cinder cleared his throat and calmly said, "Perhaps it's time that you showed them."

Her eyebrows knitted together, and she gave Cinder a look that could kill. "I don't know what you're talking about, *Cinder*," she said through clenched teeth. "And I don't want any suggestions from you."

Cinder returned her heated stare. "If you won't show them, I will."

"You wouldn't dare!"

"I will if I have to."

Grey Cloak perked up. "What are you hiding, Anya?"

"I'm not hiding anything. It's up to me to keep the secrets of the Sky Riders. I'm the last one, not you."

"I am a Sky Rider, whether you want to admit it or not. I went through the same training as everyone else." Grey Cloak's cheeks heated. He changed tactics and calmed his voice. "Anya, look around you. This is it. It's only us. If you can't trust us, you'll never be able to trust anyone."

"I don't trust you because you don't heed my advice. You want to take shortcuts and jump into portals." She wore a deep frown, but she was still beautiful. "We can't afford to take those *chances*."

"At least let me know what resources we have. Perhaps it will enlighten me, and I'll understand where you're coming from." He got closer. *Tell her what she wants to hear.* "Perhaps it will change my mind."

Anya's hard expression softened. "Don't take me for a fool." She walked away.

Grey Cloak felt the same disappointment that showed in everyone's faces. He shrugged.

Anya's strong voice echoed when she said, "Are you coming or not?"

Pleasantly surprised, the group ventured after Anya.

She led them into another section of the Safe Haven that Grey Cloak had yet to explore. It wasn't any different from the rest of the great caverns. The ground was covered in the same strange grass, brilliant flowers, and bizarre vegetation. Spring water filled a large pond that they walked by. Bright colorful fish that twinkled like fireflies dashed beneath the water's surface. The spongy bank was soft underfoot.

"It's about time," Fenora said. The grand dragon sat in the distance beside a boulder as big as she was. "I was starting to wonder if the little people would come to their senses." She eyed Anya. "Well?"

Anya searched everyone's eyes and stabbed Grey Cloak in the chest with her finger. "Don't disappoint me."

He nodded.

She gave him a wary look and turned away. She waved her hand to one side. "Do it, Fenora."

Fenora lowered her horns and set them against the boulder. The powerful muscles in her rear legs bunched, and she started pushing tons of rock across the ground.

"She's a brute," commented Streak.

"And proud of it," Feather remarked.

Fenora shoved the boulder out of the dark opening to another cave. She moved aside, revealing the full entrance. The rim of the cave mouth was decorated with stone carvings of different dragons. The images were rich in colorful minerals that accented the dragons' eyes, claws, and scales.

Anya led the way up a steep slope that led to the mouth of the cave. She stood before the massive entrance that even a grand dragon could fit through. "What you're about to see is the greatest secret of the Sky Riders. Don't you dare betray me." With that, she turned and walked into the darkness.

The moment Anya crossed the threshold, brackets of torches, high and low, flickered to life, illuminating the chamber with a vibrant orange.

Grey Cloak's jaw dropped. Dyphestive gasped. The chamber was an armory that dwarfed any Grey Cloak had ever seen. He followed Anya deeper into the chamber with an awed expression, Dyphestive right by his side.

The cut-stone walls were lined with racks of the finest weaponry he'd ever seen. There were Sky Blades with winged cross guards by the score, thunder javelins, lances, and spears. The metal of every blade caught the natural light, giving each and every weapon a life of its own.

At the base of the weapon racks were shields, some round, others rectangular, with dragon insignias stamped on the fronts. Partial-bodied mannequins stood on the stone tiles of the floor wearing suits of the Sky Riders' dragon armor. The polished partial plate mail was made up of scales that resembled dragon hide. The armor was made for all sizes, and the suits lined up to the very depths of the chamber.

"This is incredible!" Dyphestive shouted. He grabbed a

halberd that was as tall as he was and spun it around his body. Marveling, he said, "I'd like to give those Riskers a taste of this."

"Anya, this is... unbelievable. You have enough here to start an army," Grey Cloak said as he wandered deeper into the cavernous chamber. The chamber flowed into another massive room that was filled with dragon saddles, harnesses, reins, and gear. It was all crafted from the finest leather and didn't show a day of age or use. He climbed into a grand dragon saddle that lay on the ground. "I can see why you're so dug in."

She leaned against one of the decorative stone support columns. "But?"

"But we don't have enough butts to fit in the seats of these saddles or dragons to fill the harnesses for the matter," he said objectively. "We need an army. We don't have one."

"Then we'll build one someway, somehow. Now." She nodded toward the exit. "Come with me."

50

GREY CLOAK, Anya, Dyphestive, and Nath stood around a circular pedestal in the back end of the main chamber while Streak and Feather wandered about. Cinder's and Fenora's heads were lowered at the chamber's entrance.

The pedestal, holding a four-foot-wide bowl, sat on an onyx dais large enough to stand on. The pedestal itself was made of snow-white marble with gold-and-silver veins. It was covered with a cherry-colored sheet of silk that hung down to the dais.

Slowly, Anya pulled the silk sheet away. "This is the Eye of the Sky Riders."

The top of the bowl's surface was as smooth as glass. It showed a view from the clouds of Gapoli's terrain. At the moment, an image of a large lake and the surrounding land filled the picture.

Using his finger as a pointer, Grey Cloak said, "Is that Lake Flugen and Gunder Island?"

Anya nodded. "It is so, and in the present moment." She touched the glass with her hands and spread them apart. The image zoomed closer to the water, where flocks of birds skimmed over the jumping fish.

A round-eyed Dyphestive leaned over the bowl. "How is this possible?"

"My uncle, Justus, brought me here when I was very young and told me the source of its secrets. The ancient Sky Riders created the Eye by merging their powers of enchantment with the good spirits of dead dragons that still roam the skies from the ethereal plane. *This* is our biggest secret. It gives us an advantage that Black Frost doesn't know we have." She eyed them all. "And he and his brood of servants can never know. Don't tell anyone, not even your friends. This is to be kept by us."

"Can we find Zora and Talon with this?" Grey Cloak asked.

"Its power is limited. You can spend days, years, searching for a single person. It is the same as trying to find a needle in a haystack," Anya said. "Trust me, I know. I spent weeks searching for the two of you."

Grey Cloak's chest tightened. *No wonder she's mad at me.*

She caught his guilty expression and moved on. "As for your plan to return to the Wizard Watch, I'd be happy to show you why that isn't a wise idea." She moved her hand inward, manipulating the image so it zoomed out and the terrain shrank. Using one finger, she moved the picture of the world east, over the rolling hills and rich-green acres as far as the eye could see.

"That's Arrowwood, isn't it?" Dyphestive asked.

"You catch on fast." Anya cracked a smile. "You can touch it, but don't try to move it. Let me do that. Can you see the Great River now?"

They nodded.

"Good. Now we're above the Wild. Let's take a closer look at your precious tower of the Wizard Watch."

The image slowly moved downward toward leagues of land that were thick with towering trees and unmolested thickets.

A dragon rider streaked across the image.

Dyphestive leaned back. "Whoa! He looked real. Is that a Risker?"

"One of them." Anya continued to manipulate the image in the bowl. She zeroed in on not one Risker but over a score, and those were the ones in the air. They circled the Wizard Watch tower like hawks. "On the ground is an entirely different matter."

The picture hovered a hundred feet above the land surrounding the tower. The Black Guard and elven soldiers, armed to the teeth, created a thick perimeter of thousands of soldiers less than a quarter of a league from the tower. There were three rings to the army with barely the breadth of a man's shoulders between them. Chariots, horsemen, and foot soldiers waited, eager to destroy anything that came their way.

"Are you still so keen to pay the Wizard Watch a visit?" Anya crossed her arms.

Grey Cloak mulled it over. Entering the Wizard Watch was one matter. They needed a mage to enter. To make matters worse, the Riskers and an entire army would make it impossible to sneak through. He looked at Anya and smirked. "I'll think of something."

She rolled her eyes. "Here we go again."

"I have an idea," Dyphestive said. "We could sneak in."

Grey Cloak patted his brother's back. "That's the idea, but it will be impossible to avoid those troops, not to mention find a way into the tower."

Dyphestive pulled something out that was protruding from his trousers. It was the leather skull mask that belonged to the Doom Rider Scar. "But if we go disguised as Doom Riders, no one will ask questions."

Grey Cloak gave his brother a big approving smile. "Well done, brother. I like it."

"It's too risky," Anya stated.

"We'll take a vote. All in favor of impersonating Doom Riders to save the world, raise your hand." Grey Cloak and Dyphestive did so.

Anya shook her head. The three of them looked at Nath.

"What do you think?"

Nath raised his sagging scaly arm. "I like the idea. May the bold find favor over the wise."

Will Anya agree with Grey Cloak's plans?

Can they oust the underlings from the Wizard Watch?

Who is the Southern Storm and what are they really up to?

Grab Book 12 – Claws and Steel: Dragon Wars – on sale now!

And don't forget, please leave a review of Death in the Desert Book 11 when you finish. I've typed my fingers to the bone writing it and your reviews are a huge help!

DEATH IN THE DESERT REVIEW LINK

If you want to learn more about Nath and his relationship to the Underlings Verbard and Catten, check out my cross-over series Clash of Heroes! You'll love it!

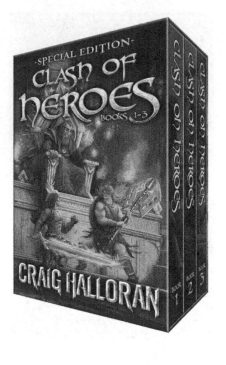

And if you haven't already, signup for my newsletter and grab 3 FREE books including the Dragon Wars Prequel.

WWW.DRAGONWARSBOOKS.COM

Teachers and Students, if you would like to order paperback copies for you library or classroom, email craig@thedarkslayer.com to receive a special discount.

Gear up in this Dragon Wars body armor enchanted with a +2 Coolness factor/+4 at Gaming Conventions. Sizes range from halfling (Small) to Ogre (XXL). LINK . www.society6.com

ABOUT THE AUTHOR

*Check me out on BookBub and follow: HalloranOn-BookBub

*I would love it if you would subscribe to my mailing list: www.craighalloran.com

*On Facebook, you can find me at The Darkslayer Report or Craig Halloran.

*Twitter, Twitter, Twitter. I am there too: www.twitter.com/CraigHalloran

*And of course, you can always email me at craig@thedarkslayer.com

See my book lists below!

OTHER BOOKS

Craig Halloran resides with his family outside his hometown of Charleston, West Virginia. When he isn't entertaining mankind, he is seeking adventure, working out, or watching sports. To learn more about him, go to www.thedarkslayer.com.

Check out all my great stories...

Free Books
> The Darkslayer: Brutal Beginnings
> Nath Dragon—Quest for the Thunderstone

The Chronicles of Dragon Series 1 (10-book series)
> The Hero, the Sword and the Dragons (Book 1)
> Dragon Bones and Tombstones (Book 2)

Terror at the Temple (Book 3)

Clutch of the Cleric (Book 4)

Hunt for the Hero (Book 5)

Siege at the Settlements (Book 6)

Strife in the Sky (Book 7)

Fight and the Fury (Book 8)

War in the Winds (Book 9)

Finale (Book 10)

Boxset 1-5

Boxset 6-10

Collector's Edition 1-10

Tail of the Dragon, The Chronicles of Dragon, Series 2 (10-book series)

Tail of the Dragon #1

Claws of the Dragon #2

Battle of the Dragon #3

Eyes of the Dragon #4

Flight of the Dragon #5

Trial of the Dragon #6

Judgement of the Dragon #7

Wrath of the Dragon #8

Power of the Dragon #9

Hour of the Dragon #10

Boxset 1-5

Boxset 6-10

Collector's Edition 1-10

The Odyssey of Nath Dragon Series (New Series) (Prequel to Chronicles of Dragon)

Exiled

Enslaved

Deadly

Hunted

Strife

The Darkslayer Series 1 (6-book series)

Wrath of the Royals (Book 1)

Blades in the Night (Book 2)

Underling Revenge (Book 3)

Danger and the Druid (Book 4)

Outrage in the Outlands (Book 5)

Chaos at the Castle (Book 6)

Boxset 1-3

Boxset 4-6

Omnibus 1-6

The Darkslayer: Bish and Bone, Series 2 (10-book series)

Bish and Bone (Book 1)

Black Blood (Book 2)

Red Death (Book 3)

Lethal Liaisons (Book 4)

Torment and Terror (Book 5)

Brigands and Badlands (Book 6)

War in the Wasteland (Book 7)

Slaughter in the Streets (Book 8)

Hunt of the Beast (Book 9)

The Battle for Bone (Book 10)

Boxset 1-5

Boxset 6-10

Bish and Bone Omnibus (Books 1-10)

CLASH OF HEROES: Nath Dragon meets The Darkslayer mini series

Book 1

Book 2

Book 3

The Henchmen Chronicles

The King's Henchmen

The King's Assassin

The King's Prisoner

The King's Conjurer

The King's Enemies

The King's Spies

The Gamma Earth Cycle

Escape from the Dominion

Flight from the Dominion

Prison of the Dominion

The Supernatural Bounty Hunter Files (10-book series)

Smoke Rising: Book 1

I Smell Smoke: Book 2

Where There's Smoke: Book 3

Smoke on the Water: Book 4

Smoke and Mirrors: Book 5

Up in Smoke: Book 6

Smoke Signals: Book 7

Holy Smoke: Book 8

Smoke Happens: Book 9

Smoke Out: Book 10

Boxset 1-5

Boxset 6-10

Collector's Edition 1-10

Zombie Impact Series

Zombie Day Care: Book 1

Zombie Rehab: Book 2

Zombie Warfare: Book 3

Boxset: Books 1-3

OTHER WORKS & NOVELLAS

The Red Citadel and the Sorcerer's Power

Made in the USA
Monee, IL
23 May 2021